A Savage and Her Wicked Ways

L. L. MOMON

If there's a book that you want to read, but it hasn't been written yet, then you must write it.

— TONI MORRISON

Trigger Warning

This book contains content that may be disturbing to some. Topics addressed include domestic violence, abuse, explicit sexual content, BDSM, consensual torture, erotic kinks, sexual assault (including rape), forced drug use, murder, and foul language. Readers discretion is advised.

Acknowledgements

Thank you God. Without you, nothing is possible. Thank you for giving me the tenacity and strength to continue when I'm weary. Thank you for providing me with patience and courage to write the things that I know may ruffle some feathers. With each book that I write, I become increasingly grateful that I have the opportunity to share the wild and vivid corners of my mind. My hope and prayer is that whatever message that I am attempting to convey is received. You all have been so supportive of me and I could never thank you enough. To my family that continue to hold me down, I want you to know that you all make the tireless nights bearable. Nigel, Eason and Asia...knowing how proud you are of me makes me wish that I could write a thousand more. To see the smile on my children's faces and to hear I'm proud of you mom makes my soul smile. To my husband, Dewayne, I love and appreciate you and your input. To my brother Sanchez, I'm so proud of you. To my auntie Dorothy, I love you and to everybody that rocks with me and you know who you are, you are doper than you will ever know.

Dedication

I dedicate this book to me and all the sisters who look, think and or act like me. Often we are misjudged in being the angry black women when that couldn't be further from the truth. We are strong and resilient and that shouldn't be looked at as a bad thing. Black women are the most overlooked and disrespected class of people in this world. If they won't look at us and respect us, it's time for us to look at ourselves and love and respect what we see in spite of what we hear. This book is for all the women who have been and are fighting tooth and nail to carve out their own little spot in this thing we call life. I want to tell you that you've got this and don't let anyone tell you that you don't.

Synopsis

Taji Dawson is a woman that lives life unapologetically on her own terms and don't give a dayum what others say. Besides her mom, her only true relationship and loyalty belongs to her best friend, Jade. Taji has been hardened by past betrayals and violent, traumatic experiences. Her trust level for men is nonexistent. In her world, men are only good for sex and money. No commitment. EVER.

Taji finds herself the target of a relentless stalker, who invades the sanctity of her home, disrupting her peace. Enters Onyx. Jade's big brother and a high-tier FBI agent. Onyx's return to Atlanta is two-fold, checking on his sister and accepting his new promotion. However, he didn't know that his first case would be close to home and personal. Vowing to uncover the stalker's identity and bring them to justice, Onyx and Taji find themselves in a dangerous game of cat and mouse.

Amidst the chaos, an unexpected bond forms between Onyx and Taji. Will he become the man to break through her icy walls and knock down the avalanche around her heart? Will he help Taji change Her Wicked Ways? In this urban fiction tale, Taji takes you on a journey of survival to one of trust and love. Her story is a testimony of resiliency and the power of healing through connection.

CHAPTER 1

Man Eater

"Lucas, if I need to turn up the intensity then just say that. I am here to facilitate your every need," Taji whispers in his ear, as she digs her stiletto heel deep into his chest. "You should know by now that whatever you wish is my command. As long as those checks keep clearing," she voices as she sucks her teeth and bites her lip. "Do you understand that, Lucas?"

"Yes, Taji, I do but I still don't get why you continue to do this. I told you that I could take you away from this, let me take care of you," he grunts, as he gazes at her freshly waxed thighs.

"Ah Ah Ah, no touching," Taji purrs while wagging her finger in his face. "I'm the only one that does the touching here. You didn't pay for that service. And take me away from what? Making filth like you suffer. Never," she laughs. "I don't know what type of bitches that you are used to dealing with, but this one doesn't need to be saved."

"Oh, come on, Taji," Lucas whines. "I'm going crazy over here. Fuck!! You feel and smell delightful. Like forreal, what is that? Coconut and shea butter or something like that?"

"Who the fuck still says *delightful* in 2025? And you do realize that all black women don't just wear coconut and shea butter. That's some racist shit, Lucas."

"I didn't mean it like that. It's just that your skin is always so smooth, and you know I love the way that you taste. Damn, Taji, I don't know how much of this shit I can stand," he protests.

"I am well-informed on how I feel and smell, Lucas. You've been telling me how irresistible I am since I've walked through that door. That's always lovely to hear but what matters is what you signed up for and dousing me with compliments wasn't it. Fyi, it's not coconut or shea butter but *Good Girl Blush* by Carolina Herrera, if you must know."

"Whatever it is, I'll buy you 10 bottles of that shit if you let me just touch you, please?"

"No! I do not want or desire your compliments. Only your money and for you to follow instructions. You didn't pay me to touch you or for you to touch me. Not tonight you didn't. You only paid for *pain* so that's exactly what you are going to get. There will be no pleasure involved unless I want otherwise."

"Well, can I change my mind on what I want?"

"No, you may not. I tried to clarify this with you when you called to set up a time and I urged you to pick your poison. You chose what you chose and that is the end of that. Now shut the fuck up before you piss me off," Taji groans as she tightens the belt around his neck, digging her heels deeper into his chest. Then she slowly trickles her heel down his body until she reaches his swollen member. Lucas squirms and grimaces from the pain as she digs the stiletto into his shaft, scraping it gently.

"Now, are you going to shut the fuck up or must I draw blood."

"Yes, Taji, yes," he grunts. "I'll shut up."

"Of course you will," she confirms as she removes the heel from his groin. Taking two steps forward, she postures herself directly over his face, making sure that he gets a nice view of her glistening pussy lips.

"Damn, Taji, that pussy is so fat. Why are you doing this to me? Please let me taste it. I will give you whatever you want. Just name it," he entreats.

"Don't piss me off. Please just shut the fuck up, Lucas... you are not to say another word or there will be consequences," she commands before dropping down and hovering her pussy over his nose. She sways back and forth to ensure that he gets a good whiff of what he is forbidden from enjoying.

The tantalizing aroma from Taji's nectar nearly sends Lucas into a tailspin, which is exactly what she expected to happen. He struggles to lift his head but is unsuccessful due to the strap that surrounds his body, rendering him virtually helpless. He continues to stick out his stiff, salivating tongue, desperate for a taste but fails miserably. Unbeknownst to him, Taji has performed this tactic enough times to have it perfected. She knows just how far down to hover to avoid contact.

"Taji, this is literally torture. I'm aware that I paid for pain, but I thought that it would be physical pain. This is straight up *agony*. A psychological mind fuck and I don't know if I am equipped to handle this. Will you untie me please? Please... just let me taste one drop," he pleads but to no avail.

Instead of lowering her sweet spot to allow his tongue to reach, she slaps him across the face and tightens the belt another loop. Damn near cutting off his air-flow until he taps out. "You don't have a choice, Lucas. I thought you understood the rules here. See, that's your white privilege talking. Thinking that you have a say. You don't run shit here because I am in charge. You are not. I decide what I will let you do and taste. However, I'm feeling quite generous today."

"We have 10 more minutes left in this session," she advises as she unloosens and removes the belt from his neck. "I think I'll leave it up to you to decide what's done during that time. Would you like for me to straddle your face and glide my wet pussy across your nose and mouth? Shall I bounce up and down on your dick like a see-saw? Or would you like for me to beat the shit out of you until you beg me to stop? Which will it be, Lucas?"

"Please, just let me——" Taji cuts him off mid-sentence by forcefully lowering her pussy to his mouth, smothering him a tad before she relaxes and let nature take its course. Lucas doesn't waste any time. Finally, he gets to do the very thing that he's been begging for, taste her essence. He sucks and licks her clit with such passion and eagerness.

Each lick feels phenomenal. It's clear as day that she's super aroused. Lucas's chin is practically drenched from her nectar. Yet, she acts completely bored and uninterested. Moans desperately attempt to escape her mouth, but she doesn't dare give him the pleasure. Regardless of the climax that is sure to erupt in no time, she still doesn't falter. Instead, she bites down on her lip and silences her pleasure sounds.

Making men grovel at her feet brings Taji unspeakable

joy. She has an unusual talent. Not only is she smart and beautiful, she possesses the innate ability to take one look at the male species and conclude just what it would take to siphon anything she wants from them. This is and has always been her end game. Give them 10% of yourself while requiring 110% from them.

This is a philosophy that she lives by and never strays from, no matter what these men present. This feat has been quite easy for her. In her 33 years of living, she has yet to meet one soul that made her want to deviate from this plan.

In Taji's mind, all men are simpletons and could not be trusted by any stretch of the imagination. The only thing that they could be entrusted to do is *hurt and damage you*. She's convinced that all men are liars and dogs by nature, so they are just fulfilling their purpose in life, being trifling, dog ass niggas.

Her beliefs are that men are incapable of being faithful and they all cheat. She has no unrealistic expectations. There are no illusions of grandeur and that's what sets her apart from most women. She sees them for what she thinks they are and makes no excuses for it.

Taji swears that love is overrated and to give your heart to a nigga is crazy business. Preposterous even.

There is not a man walking this earth that she deemed

worthy of making her deviate from her philosophy that men aren't shit and she isn't looking for his ass either.

Taji leaves Lucas's high-rise apartment with a fatter wallet and a partially satisfied twat. The tongue lashing she received only served as an hors d'oeuvres in comparison to her insatiable sexual appetite. She wrecks her brain, trying to decide on which lucky gentleman will get the pleasure of enjoying her unsolicited company tonight and finishing her off. *Ahh, decisions, decisions*, she thought.

Granted, she has a man lying in her bed at her luxurious home. One that is willing and waiting to do whatever she asks, but that is not who she intends to enjoy tonight. Taji has chiseled out her life in such a way that enables her to pick and choose who she deals with and when. Taji stands 5'8" with legs that seem to go on forever. Big perky boobs, a small waist, with a natural, super thick phat ass.

She has long and wavy hair that dances with the top of her ass crack. Beautiful dark caramel skin and big doe like eyes.

She looks completely exotic, but according to her ancestry DNA, she's a straight up black woman. People always stopped and asked her what she was mixed with, which she always found offensive and would simply say, "African and American," and walk the fuck away. That's the type of bitch Taji is. *Pretty privilege* is definitely a thing because it gets her just about everything she wants.

Taji has a roster of men of every caliber to choose from. For instance, there is Malcolm, a short quick tempered account executive who has a thing for bossing women around. Malcom has a serious Napoleon complex. While in her reality or any other world, she would never date or even take a second glance at such an individual. However, he has a mean head game and will suck the fart out her ass if she requested. She let him think he was in charge. Especially when he said things like, "Cum in my mouth and piss on my neck." She was happy to oblige. Pissing on men made Taji feel like she was uplifting the entire female species. After all, they piss on us *figuratively* every chance they got. It was only fitting that she returned the favor.

Or should she summon Rico, a Sergeant in the military? Rico is a tall statue of a man with grey eyes and has a strut that rivals Denzel Washingtons in *Malcolm X*. He is a

Puerto Rican Papi from up north, who appears rough around the edges but is a gentle giant. He is that 90's fine and his swag stops traffic. His looks demand attention and people sit and deliberate on where this fine specimen of a man came from. Rico can put it down in the bedroom for sure. The main drawback for her is his career, which comes first, leaving Taji the possibility of being second and she wouldn't dare have that. Thus, the reason that he is used strictly for dick and a quick cuddle afterwards.

Then we have Motion. The high-level drug dealer from the southside who keeps her laced. He never shows up empty handed and always comes bearing expensive gifts. Diamonds are his favorite. He bought her a one-of-a-kind Richard Millie watch, worth almost a million dollars, and a custom Lamborghini that she never drives because she doesn't like the attention that it brings her. These other street niggas out here wasn't fucking with Motion in the tricking department and all he wanted is a bad bitch on his side.

He had one in Taji. She was all for that until the day he took her on a high-speed chase in an attempt to elude the police. She wasn't with that jail shit, so from that moment on, he became a moment in black history. Except for those times when she craves that thug loving. That *snatch your lace front off and slap you in the back of the head* kind of loving. Other than that, it is pretty much curtains for him.

Next up, there is Farod. Farod owns a string of gas stations and restaurants. The word on the street is that his family is worth billions. He probably is a bigger trick than Motion but in lieu of tangible gifts, Farod pays big bills. Taji requested that her mortgage be paid off and all of her bills transferred to his autopay. He quickly obliged.

All that he requires from her is to come by and visit the store or restaurant at least once a week, swooning and doting on him as if she was his woman. His goal is to make his big brother jealous. Farod has a wife at home that he claims to love dearly. His brother has a wife as well but also has a beautiful side chick. In true little brother fashion, he wanted one, too. So Taji jumped at the chance once she found out what he was offering. Quick and easy dividends.

Last but not least, we have Chosen. The man that lies in Taji's bed night after night, wishing that she would come to her senses and realize that he's *the one* for her. Chosen is truly one of a kind. He's handsome, has a great sense of humor, empathetic, in tune with his feelings, considerate, hard-working, masculine yet taps into his feminine energy when needed, well endowed, polite, kind, witty, intelligent, compromising, loves his mama, thoughtful, responsible, wealthy, honest, and trustworthy.

He has nothing but good intentions towards Taji. Chosen is a regular chick's fantasy. He is literally everything that a woman could ask for in a man and even still, she doesn't trust him enough to settle down.

Chosen has been the only man that has ever set foot into Taji's personal space. She loves having him at her beck and call. He is always there when she wants and needs him. He provides her with the strong sense of security that every woman craves. Even when they claim that they don't. Taji rips and runs the streets daily and comes home to a fine, chocolate, bowlegged, rugged man's man.

Chosen has his own home, several actually, and many properties. However, he prefers to spend most of his nights at Taji's house. She doesn't protest because while she's in these streets doing her thang, she loves having a man at home waiting on her. She adores the fact that he has her bath water ready when she walks through the door and her pajamas laid out. Chosen has OCD so he keeps the house in impeccable order. He cares for her miniature poodle, Bella, while she's away and is just all-around, *That Nigga*.

The household runs smoothly with him around. He's her companion and house manager if you will but she treats him like he's disposable. Is it right? No. Does Taji care? Again, no.

Chosen knew what he was dealing with when he agreed to get involved with Taji. She was very forthcoming about not wanting a serious relationship and only desired a friend with benefits. She gets everything else she wants from the other men, so she didn't want anything but someone to chill with after a long day of galivanting/whoring.

According to Chosen, he was cool with that as well because he'd just ended a 7-year relationship. At the time, he wasn't looking for anything serious either. He thought it was a win-win. He assumed that he was getting a beautiful, super secure, independent woman that would fuck his brains out. Then turn around and binge watch a Netflix series. Nothing serious. A homie-lover-friend. That sounds great, right? Wrong!! He fell in love with Taji within three weeks of spending time with her, as most of them do. He didn't know what hit him until it was too late, and he's been hooked like a fiend ever since.

CHAPTER 3

Big Mama

A s Taji trots into the parking lot of Lucas's complex, her phone begins ringing and vibrating. *Big Mama* by Latto signifies that her bestie, Jade, is on the line.

"What's up, Big Mama? What you got going on?" Taji says as she retrieves her key fob from her Dior saddle bag.

"Girl, nothing. Just trying to see where you are and what you were doing. I could use a little company. I've got some shit going on and I could sure use my bestie to lift my spirits. Your ass is always a vibe," Jade utters.

"I'm just leaving Lucas's spot and was on a mission to finish getting my socks knocked off. What's wrong, Boo? Is it that tired ass nigga, Teef, again?" Taji queries.

Jade falls silent.

"Jade, if it is, I don't even care to talk about it because

it's not going to do anything but piss me off. I'll come chill with you and do whatever you need for me to do but please don't bring his ass up while I'm there. I hate to get in your house and tear some shit up. Plus, just saying his name gives me the damn hives. I still don't see what you see in him but whatever," Taji scoffs.

"Ok, okay. I won't say shit about him then. Just come through please. I'll be waiting on you. Just use your key to let yourself in and while you're at it, can you stop by the liquor store and get us something to sip on? I could use a shot or two."

"No problem," Taji expresses. Popping her lips, she chirps, "I'll be there in a little bit," she says as she cranks her BMW 8 series Gran Coupe with the speakers blaring in the background. "Damn, Jade, my bad. I didn't realize that I had the music up so loud. Anyway, see you in a little bit."

"Thank you again, Taji. I appreciate you," she grumbles in a melancholy voice as she hangs up the phone.

Taji couldn't understand for the life of her what Jade sees in Teef. Teef isn't his birth given name. Reggie is, but Taji calls him Teef because he has an overbite that enters the room before he does. Jade is gorgeous. Her complexion always reminded Taji of the butter pecan ice cream that she would see her mother eat as a child. Jade stands 5'5". Busty, with thick thighs and with the ass and hips to match. She attempts to dressed modestly in order to conceal that wagon that she's dragging under those sanctified dresses that she wore. Jade and Taji were roommates in college. They both majored in Biomedical science. Jade is the quiet, sheltered, reserved, southern bell from a small town with only two traffic lights. Taji is the adventurous, extrovert wild child, also from a small town but had a lot more experience with life than Jade did.

Jade wasn't into the nightlife and kept her head in her books as her mother and father had instructed. She often stayed back at the dorm room while Taji partied until the sun came up. After months of living together, Taji was able to pull her out of her shell just a little but never tried to change who she was.

Jade liked Taji because she never made her feel like a lame. She wasn't wild and didn't care for clubs and drinking all night. It wasn't her thing. In high school, Jade was constantly picked on because her parents were strict. They didn't allow her to hang out with friends or attend any dances or parties. Not even the prom. Taji never picked on her and made sure that she understood that she didn't have to do anything that she didn't feel comfortable doing.

Taji favored Jade for the same reason. She could be herself around her. She never felt judged by her even though she probably deserved to be. Jade spent countless nights nursing Taji back to health after those drunken nights. When Taji was sexually assaulted at a party, Jade never left her side. Taji never forgot how safe she felt with her. She became a positive role model and helped Taji stick to her guns when it came to school. Without her, Taji would have definitely failed.

They became thick as thieves and the rest is history. They both received their degrees from Alabama State University and vowed to stay close to one another no matter what. They both moved to black Hollywood - Atlanta, Georgia - to begin their careers. Jade married Teef eight years ago and has excelled in her career. She carries the title of Deputy Medical Examiner for Clayton County, Georgia and as you can guess, her hands are full.

Taji, on the other hand, never worked in her field at all. In fact, she's never worked a day in her life. Why would she? Fresh out of college, she received a hefty lump sum of money from her ex-baller boyfriend once they split. He didn't want Taji to expose all his dirty little secrets, so he rewarded her silence with a five million dollar payoff as long as she signed his NDA. She took the money, invested some, spent a lot, and has lived like a queen ever since. Which isn't hard to do because all of her bills are on someone else's auto pay and her mortgage has been paid in full.

She stops at the drive through liquor store to acquire

four bottles of Cabernet Sauvignon and a fifth of Casamigos Blanco. Taji doesn't know what Teef did this time. Whatever it is, Taji plans on getting Jade so fucked up that she doesn't remember.

The loot has been secured so she gets on the freeway and heads towards Jade's subdivision. She decides to give Chosen a courtesy call to let him know that she will be out later than expected. To her, communication is of the utmost importance and she doesn't believe in leaving people hanging.

"Chosen baby, I'm going to head over to a friend's house for a little bit. I'm letting you know so that you don't wait up for me. She's going through some things with her trifling ass man, so I may be awhile," she advises.

"Taji, this is the 3rd night in a row that you've stayed out late. You told me last night that you would work on returning home at a decent hour. What happened to that promise?"

"I didn't promise you anything, Chosen... I said that I would work on it and I am. My friend needs me and I'm going to be there for her. Just like I would be for you."

"Shit, you not getting it. I do need you, Taji. I want you to come home. You don't always have to be in the streets. Them muthafuckas ain't going nowhere. They will be there. I may not."

Taji looks around in her car like *I know this mutha-fucka didn't* before putting him in his place.

"I don't give a fuck, Chosen. Don't be there then. No one is holding you hostage. If you are growing weary of waiting on me, I get it. Hell, you can leave anytime you get ready, and I will completely understand. Just make sure to leave my keys on the entry table and lose my number. There is no doubling back either so if you are done, make sure you're done," she gripes before hanging up the phone.

"He must not know who he's fucking with. Talking about leaving. Leave then nigga!!!" she yells to herself, as she turns into Jade's quiet subdivision.

CHAPTER 4

Teef's Secret

A s Taji grabs the brown paper sack full of goodies, her phone dings and a text message from Chosen comes through. She peeks at the name, smacks her lips, and continues getting out of the car. Her hands are full so she cannot dig in her bag for her keys, so she rings the doorbell. Teef answers.

"Well, hello there, Taji. What did we do to deserve such a visit this late at night?....Ohhh, and you come bearing gifts. How nice of you," he quips while rolling his eyes.

"Umm, Reggie, are you going to let me in or not? You see me standing here with this heavy ass bag and you didn't even offer to take it for me. Oh, and I don't know what you did to my sister but I'm about to find out. She better not tell me that you did no fuck shit either. Just know, she and I both are tired of your shit, Reggie. I don't want to have to call the calvary for your ass but I will."

Teef closes the door in Taji's face. A few seconds later, she sees Jade's shadow darken the door. She opens it, apologizing for her husband's manners.

"Oh girl, it's cool. Don't apologize for him. You didn't do shit to apologize for. The only thing you did wrong was marry that FUCK NIGGA!!" she yells. "You can tell that his mammy didn't raise him right. That's the reason why he ain't shit til' this day!!!" she screams over Jade's shoulder as Teef disappears from their sight.

"Oooh, girl, I really can't stand that nigga. Any of these niggas for that matter. See, shit like that is why I stay single. It ain't no way in hell that I would be able to deal with attitudes and bullshit like that on a daily basis. I would have been in jail. Anyway, hey, Boo," Taji grins as she side hugs Jade. "Where should I take our goodies?"

"Just follow me. We are going to the guest house so that we can have some privacy. I don't need Reggie to hear anything that I'm about to say."

"This must be serious, Jade. We never go out there," Taji affirms as she picks up the pace to catch up with her.

"Ummm, Jade. Are we supposed to drink this shit out of our hands? You didn't bring any glasses from inside the house?"

"Bitch, I'm 2 steps ahead of you. I have buckets of ice, a bottle opener, and plenty of glasses in this guest house."

"Well, I wouldn't know. We never come out here but I'm glad to know you are prepared."

They trek down the walkway and arrive at the guesthouse. Jade opens the door and before Taji could close it behind her, tears erupt from Jade's eyes.

"Awww, hell nawl, Jade!" Taji exclaims. "What's wrong? Talk to me," she says as she opens the Casamigos and searches for the shot glasses. "Go on over there to that couch and sit down. I'm going to fix us a couple of shots and you start talking in the meantime."

"I want to tell you, but you told me not to talk about *him*," Jade cries.

"Girl, don't pay my ass no attention. I was just talking shit. You can talk to me about whatever you want."

"That nigga is cheating on me again," Jade blurts out. "I know he is. My PH has been off for some weeks now, so I went to the doctor and they told me that I had Chlamydia. I made them do a full blood work panel to be sure that the bastard didn't give me anything else, but yep, Taji, he did it again," she says while sobbing into her hands.

"Awww, Jade. I'm so sorry. I really am. I hate that you are going through this again. I'm not going to say I told you so because that is not what you need right now. What I want to know is what are you going to do?"

"Wait, that's not it, Taji," she says while looking down at her wedding ring.

"Ok, wait, wait. You've got to take me one fuck up at a time." Taji tells her as she walks over and hands her a shot and the bottle.

"I know it's a lot to take in but I want to get this shit all out. I believe that it's a *man* that he's fucking with."

Taji stares at her without saying a word. Trying to find the kindest, most unoffensive way to say what she's thinking. She comes up with nothing, so she blurts out. "You mean to tell me *that* dick in the booty ass nigga is *really* a *dick in the booty ass* nigga. I mean, not figuratively but *literally?*"

They stare at each other for a moment and then burst out laughing.

"See, I knew that even though I'm hurting like hell, I could always count on you to make me feel better. And yes, Taji. That's exactly what I mean."

"So, are you going to tell me how we arrived at this conclusion? Like, did you see something? Did you find some dirty text messages or videos with him and his lil boyfriend getting freaky?"

"No, nothing like that. He's way too smooth to get caught that way. I found a butt plug, lube, a cock ring, and a dildo in a box that he had hidden away in the attic. I think he put it there because he knows that I hate getting on that ladder. It's so small and I wasn't sure that it would hold my chunky ass. Anytime I needed something out of there, I would send him to get it."

"I wanted to get the Thanksgiving decorations from the attic, but he wasn't home. I couldn't send the maid because she refused to do it as well. I did what I had to do and climbed my big ass up that ladder and it was sitting in a box in the corner. I thought that it was some of the things that I'd packed away last year but to my surprise, a big shiny butt plug fell out and so did I."

"Jade, I wish I could say that I was surprised but I can't. It's hard to shock me these days. Especially since we live in Hotlanta. All these niggas are suspect if you ask me. Let me play devil's advocate for a second and before you ask, yes, I'm on your side. I'm *always* on your side."

"Now, you know that I've just about done it all and seen it all. Men's prostates are in their asses and from what they tell me, it's nothing like a regular orgasm. Apparently, it is 10 times better. Just because he has butt plugs doesn't necessarily mean that he's gay. He could just like the pleasure that it brings. Has he ever asked you to peg him before?"

"Girl, what the hell is pegging?"

"It's using a strap on a man. Women do it all the time with their husbands. That's if he's into that kind of thing of course. A lot of men love it but are ashamed to admit it to their wives so they do it themselves. He could just like ass-play. It doesn't mean he's gay."

"Well, how do you explain the dildo having 2 sides to it? Like a double dong dildo. Are you about to tell me that he has two assholes too?"

"AHHHH... HAHAHAHAH!!!" Taji screams with laughter. She's so tickled that she can't get her words out. Stammering, "Ummm... ummmm... You're right, sis. I can't explain that one away. Welp, so much for trying to see his side of things. That nigga is gay as a two-dollar bill. Which is fine, except for the fact that he's your husband. So now I ask you again. What are you going to do?"

"I want to confront him and let him know that I found his little stash of nasties and of course tell him that he gave me a VD, but I don't know where to start."

"I know you want to go in that house and let it rip but please don't do that. Men, especially powerful men, have all kind of fucked up kinks. Trust me, I know, and they will go to great lengths to keep their secret. I don't want him trying to harm you in any way. Would you like to know what I think you should do?"

"Please tell me because I'm lost."

"I want you to move in silence. Like, *literally*... let him go to work one day and come home to an empty ass house. You never tell a nigga like that, that you are leaving. I watch too much ID network to ever make that mistake.

You've got to move in silence and a woman in your position can do it. You've got the money."

"Yes, I do have the money but what if he tries to fight me and they freeze my account or some shit like that?"

"We will cross that bridge when we get there. Shit, if I were you, I'd go buy a new house and move clean the fuck across town. Leave his ass high and dry. Then divorce his ass and drain him for every drop that he can spare. You are in good graces with all the lawyers, doctors, and county officials. I know you would come out on the winning side because you don't deserve any less."

"Taji, I'm glad to see that someone has some faith in this situation. I'm drained and so tired."

"You've put up with his shit for a long time and whether you know it or not, you've got the upper hand. You can make a clean break."

"You are making it sound so easy, Taji, but we've got a lot of things to consider."

"Like what, Jade? You don't have any children with his ass and the only thing that you own together is this house, right?"

"Wrong," Jade murmurs while looking embarrassed and scrunching her nose.

"What the hell else do you two have together?"

"A house in his hometown, Alexander City. We own a lake house on Lake Martin. We bought it right after we got married. I didn't mention it to you because I didn't think it was a big deal."

"It's not a big deal when you have a faithful husband and you all are staying together but that isn't the case is it? It's only a big deal now because that just adds another layer that you have to cut through. Do you have any lawyer friends that you can call?"

"I do but they are his friends too, Taji. That's what makes this thing feel so difficult. Our lives are so intertwined that it's going to be hard to get around it. I mean, at this point, I don't know who I can trust."

"Fuck all that. I've got plenty of connections, so you don't worry about that. Just pour up another shot. Tonight, we get shitfaced, and we will conquer the rest another day. Just stay away from that son of a bitch for now. You are going to move in silence. Okay, Jade?'

"Ok," Jade agrees.

CHAPTER 5

Disposable

"Now, do you see why I will *never* give my all or my heart to these dudes? You've got to remember that your heart has one function. It is to pump blood and oxygen to and from your organs. Nothing more or less. Feelings should be left out of it. Listening to your heart will lead you to do ignorant shit like actually take these men seriously. Or even worse, fall in love and that is definitely a **hard no** for me."

"Taji. You've got to give someone a real shot someday, right?"

"I did. I tried that love shit once and it was overrated. In 2013, at the tender age of 22, I decided that I never wanted to experience that kind of hurt again in this lifetime. That was the first *and* last time I slid down anyone's wall over a nigga. I learned real quick that if you let your guard down, they will only embarrass you and I refuse to give them the opportunity again."

"Jade, this is why I get what I can from them and move on."

"I will never suffer at the hands of another man. Never. The only thing that is suffering around these parts are them and their wallets. *Fuck you, pay me* is my motto! If I were to ever get married, it would be strictly for money, not love." Taji exclaims.

For the rest of the night they drink, laugh, and reminisce until neither one can stand.

"Oh, shit. I meant to read the text message from Chosen. Girl, I've been so wrapped up in your shit that I forgot about my own. Mine is trivial compared to what you are going through but let me see what this nigga is talking about."

Chosen: For weeks, I've been thinking about our relationship. Or whatever this is that we've got going on. I tried to hang in there Taji because I told myself a long time ago that you were worth waiting for. However, the way that you talked to me tonight lets me know that you don't value me at all. You didn't even try to compromise. You told me what you were and were not going to do and that was the end of it. It's been 3 years and I'm tired of putting my life on hold for you. I want a wife, kids, and a family. Shit that you have no interest in. I don't mean to write a paragraph on your phone, but this was the best way to do this because we both know that you are stubborn and refuse to listen to anyone else's point of view but your own. You know Google will tell you that a diamond is the hardest substance on earth. But I think they've got it wrong. It should say Taji's heart. I hope that someone, someday, can penetrate that diamond in your chest because I obviously couldn't. In short. I'm gone. I've gathered all my things from your home and I'm out. Have a nice life Taji.

"Girl, what the hell?" Taji mumbles.

"What is it? Tell me."

"Girl, it is Chosen telling me that he's leaving. Like I really give a damn. Apparently, he thinks I'm hard to deal with, inconsiderate, and self-centered. I'm drunk and a drunk man/woman, tells no lies. I'm gonna be real with you and myself. He's right, but it's not like he just met me. I've been like this for years."

"Maybe he thought you would change for him." Jade voices.

"Maybe he did but that was his own mistake. I guess he figured out that I'm not changing for anyone. You either take me like I am or kick rocks. Hell, I've never tried to change him."

"Well, if we are being honest, Taji, there is nothing to change. That man is damn near perfect. I've always liked him for you. I think you two could do big things together, but *you don't want a relationship*," she mouths in a mimicking voice.

"Shut your drunk ass up. I know you are talking crazy if you are talking about togetherness. Togetherness my ass," Taji slurs. "I'm not trying to have none of that shit and Chosen knew that when we started dealing with each other. Not to be funny but look at the situation that you are in."

"This is exactly what I want to avoid. Too much bullshit comes with trying to hold a nigga down. They make you think that everything is good and then **bam**. You're getting fucked in the ass. No pun intended." Taji giggles.

"So are you not going to go home and see if he's really gone? If he is still there, you could try to talk it out."

"There's nothing to talk about, Jade. It sounds like he's made his mind up, so who am I to try to change it? Anyhow. Where is the fleece blanket that I love to snuggle under when I'm over here?"

"It's in the house but there is one in the closet just like it. Are you going to sit here and tell me that you really don't give a damn about that man leaving?"

"Yes, that's exactly what I'm going to tell you because I don't. Now, I'm tired and sleepy. Are you staying out here with me or are you going in the house with fruity booty?" They both snicker like two little schoolgirls.

"Stooooop... Taji. That's not nice. And yes. You said to act normal so I'm gonna go in the house and go straight to bed. That's if I can make it up those stairs. That Casamigos has got me gone. I know that I'm going to have a headache in the morning."

"Girl, everybody knows that you are a complete lightweight. A wine cooler gets you fucked up, so I know that Casamigos is going to take you down through the valley. Anyway, good night, sis. I'll probably be gone already when you wake up so in case I don't see you, give me a hug and I'll call you tomorrow."

They hug before Jade leaves the guest house and Taji reminds her not to stray from the plan. No matter how much she wants to let it out, don't. Jade agrees, kisses her on the cheek, and leaves.

The next morning, bright and early and barely sober, Taji takes off, heading home to an empty house. She was three sheets to the wind when she read Chosen's message last night, but now the reality of him being gone starts to sink in, and it is not at all what she suspected. Sadness begins to creep upon her on her drive home. She pulls into her driveway and opens her garage. Once she sees that Chosen's car is absent, sadness stops creeping and hits her like a ton of bricks.

She enters her home and finds Bella. She starts the coffee maker then lets her out. She hurries upstairs to the closet to see if Chosen's clothes are gone and they are. Once Bella finishes doing her business, she lets her back in and pours herself a cup of coffee. She doesn't have to feed Bella. Chosen bought her an automatic feeder and water bowl to ensure that she never goes hungry. He is thoughtful like that.

She ascends back upstairs to the master bedroom. She hadn't paid attention before but out of her peripheral vision, she notices a small box. A piece of paper lies underneath that reads:

I know that you have more than enough diamond rings, but this one was supposed to mean more than all of them put together. Whether you know it or not, I loved you and intended on making you my wife, but I see now that you will never be wifey material. I've put my life on hold long enough waiting for you to see what was right in front of you all along. Love. I have made peace with not being the one for you and I am moving on. I didn't hurt you and I don't know who did. My advice to you is to go somewhere and heal. Get some help. It's obvious that you are running from something and whatever it is will hold you captive, if you don't confront it. I wish you the best of luck in your future endeavors and I pray that you find the most important person of all. Yourself.

Best Regards,
Chosen

PUTTING THE LETTER DOWN, she grabs and slips on the pajamas that Chosen laid at the foot of the bed for her.

As she sips her coffee, she couldn't help but think about the care that he put into things to make sure that she was pleased. She grabs Bella and cuffs her in her arms. She looks around at the bedroom and realizes that he really erased every trace of himself from the room. There are no remnants of Chosen. It's as if he never existed in her world.

Only Taji's essence remains. This is certainly the way that she preferred things beforehand but for the first time in a long time, she wonders if this may be her downfall. Selfishness. Her head starts to throb, so she lets it. Thinking that maybe she deserves to feel the pain. Maybe it's needed to bring her back to reality a tad. She lies there thinking about the maybes until sleep finds her.

CHAPTER 6

Papers

Taji is awakened by the slobbery kisses of her furbaby, alerting her that someone was at the door. Getting up, she descends downstairs to give whoever is on the other side a piece of her mind. Because why are they knocking like the police and an even better question than that, why didn't they call before dropping by? She glances at the clock on the wall, it reads 6:08 P.M. She practically slept the day away.

As she approaches the door, she stops in her tracks, thinking, *I knew his ass would come to his senses and come back. Chosen knows that he can't live without me.* She thought wrong. Taji opens the door to find Jade standing in the rain with a suitcase and duffel bag. It appears that she has been in some sort of a scuffle. Her wig is cocked to the side and disheveled can't even begin to describe the way her friend looks.

"Girl, what in the hell happened to you?" Taji queries. "You better not tell me that bastard put his hands on you."

"Quite the contrary," Jade admits. "I beat his ass for the old and the new and he told me that he was going to call the police on me. I grabbed what I could and left. Can I please stay with you until I can figure out my next move? Girl, I'm all fucked up over this."

"Anyone would be, Jade. You are only human," Taji concurs.

She invites her in, and Jade stands in the foyer weeping. Soaked from head to toe, Taji's heart hurts for her friend. She's such a good person with a kind heart. Taji finds it sad that more often than not, women are viewed as *weak* or *doormats* when they love as hard as someone like Jade does. They are not. They are doing what their nature tells them to do. Love, nurture, and forgive. Her only mistake is loving a man that was never equipped to return the love that she offered. As she listens to her friend's cries, she feels nothing but empathy and sorrow.

"I know that you told me not to say anything, but I just couldn't help it. I tried my best to go to sleep last night and as drunk as I was, I still couldn't rest my mind. I tossed and turned all night and when he got up this morning to get ready for work, I could barely stand to look at him."

"I went to work, and he was home when I got there. I couldn't take it anymore. He was too damn comfortable for me. It irked my nerves that he obviously has no remorse for what he's done. He was sitting in that recliner looking like Buckie the damn beaver and I let it rip. I didn't mention the gay thing but I sure as hell couldn't sit on the Chlamydia thing any longer. That muthafucka had the nerve to try and touch me intimately after I'd just told him that I had Chlamydia. I snapped."

"You? Snapped? What did you say, friend?" Taji asks as she leans in, ready for all the hot tea to be spilled.

"I told him that he would *never* ever get to touch me like that again. Because of him, I am walking around with a tainted pussy and that isn't right, Taji," she wails as she falls into Taji's arms. "I've been a good wife to that bastard. I don't deserve this."

"You sure the fuck don't," Taji mutters as she holds her and comforts her. Letting her go, Taji grabs Jade's bags and takes them to the guest room. A sobbing Jade follows her and they have a seat on the bed.

"First of all, you know damn well that you can stay here. You didn't even have to ask. You take as long as you need to figure this shit out. In the meantime, I've got you."

"Taji, were you able to call any of your contacts today? Like your lawyer friends? I want to get the ball rolling on this divorce thing as quickly as possible."

"No, sweetie, I haven't. I've been asleep and lying around since I got home but I'll start calling around now. Just give me a minute to take a bath and get myself together. You should do the same. Now go in my closet and pick out some comfy clothes to wear around the house and I will call your job for you and let them know that you need to take a few days off for personal matters."

"Taji, no. I can't do that. I need to go to work. They won't know what to do without me there. Trust me. That place turns into a shitshow when I'm away."

"Well today is the day that those fuckers learn. You've got to take care of yourself and your business. Fuck that job. I promise you that those dead people will still be there waiting for you when you get back. They have nowhere to be." Taji stares at Jade, grins, and cackles.

"You get on my nerves so bad, Taji, but I love you to death. You are my sister from another mister."

"Speaking of sisters, have you talked to yours?" Taji questions with a raised eyebrow.

"Girl, hell no. I don't want them coming down here trying to burn the city down about lil old me. That is a problem that none of us need."

"Well what about your big brother, Onyx? I'm sure that he would want to know how his baby sister is doing. I hadn't heard you mention him in so long."

"Taji, you have no idea how much I miss my brother.

If I had to tell anyone, it would be him. Even though we were furthest apart in age. We were closer than my sisters and I were. Probably because they were always getting in trouble and being sent away. He was the good boy, the golden child. Onyx used to take me everywhere with him. I was like his own little personal babydoll. It was all good until he joined the FBI. That put a serious strain on our relationship. He's never around anymore and I barely see him."

"I understand that you miss him, Jade, but that's an even better reason to contact him and let him know what's going on with you. You know that he loves you and your sisters do, too. Sapphire and Diamond play no games when it comes to you. You know, now that I think about it, why did your parents give all four of you stripper names and expect you all to act like saints? Huh, make it make sense. I still wonder that til' this day. You know what else I wonder? How are you, Sapphire, and Diamond light-skinned and Onyx is dark skinned? He must have gotten his color from your daddy and you and the thugs got their color from your mama. Is that what happened?"

"I don't know, Taji, why don't you ask them since you wanna know so bad?"

"No thanks, I'll pass. They aren't about to douse me with holy water and pour oil on me trying to deliver me from my trifling ways, as your mama used to say. That

woman took one look at me and new my ass wasn't shit."
Taji says while cackling to herself. "And I dare not ask the
thugs anything. They not about to lay hands on me."

"Seriously though, I may just call Sapphire and
Diamond and see if they will come over for a girls' weekend," Taji laughs as if she's joking but she's really not.
"Doesn't that sound like fun, Jade? Your big sisters and me
together should definitely get you out of that funk. We
used to have a ball together."

"Taji, please no. You know those girls aren't wrapped
too tight. One would douse Reggie's ass with gasoline and
the other would strike a match. I'll pass on the BBQ of my
ex-husband to be."

"Shidd, you will but I won't. I'll bring the potato salad
and the baked beans," Taji giggles as she chews air.

"I'm forreal, Taji. Sapphire just got off papers this year
and Diamond has to mess up one more time before she
goes away for good. The judge told her that she better not
ever see her in that courtroom again. She called my sister *a
menace to society*. I'm not about to put their freedom on
the line. I don't want them going back because of me."

"Jade, we don't have to tell them about what's going
on with you. I just think that it would do you good to see
some familiar faces in a loving setting. I can call my home-
girls, too. I know that Luna and Kirsten would be down."

"Maybe in few days or maybe next week. For now, I

just need to get my mental together before I deal with anyone."

"Boooooo, tomatoes, tomatoes, tomatoes. You are no fun, but I completely get it, friend. Anyway, heartbreak is the worst. I'm going to give you some time to yourself and go wash yesterday off my ass. Then I will make a few calls. You get comfortable and do whatever you need to do to feel better. I've got some business to handle later on tonight so I may be gone for awhile if everything checks out."

"I bet your freaky ass does."

"It's not like that. I'm just going by to see a friend. That's all. No sex will be involved, I don't think." Taji giggles and sashays out of the guest room.

Jade lies across the bed thinking about her family unit as a whole. Her mother had three girls and one boy named Onyx. All of which were raised to do the right thing but she was the only one of the girls that didn't go down the wrong path. Jade was absolutely right in not wanting her sisters involved. They would for sure set this little city on fire. Sapphire had been to prison for attempted murder times two. She came home and caught her boyfriend with another woman. Crashing out, she left the woman in critical condition and her boyfriend was in ICU for months.

Her boyfriend's face was unrecognizable. She stabbed him four times and bashed his head in with a cast iron skillet. She didn't stab the girl, but she beat her so badly that she was in a full body cast for months. This happened when she was barely 20 years old and she's 38 now. She's been in and out of the system since her teenage years and spent 15 years in prison because of that crime. She's out and doing well and Jade wants to keep it that way.

Diamond had her trouble with the law as well. When Diamond was 24, she went out on a date with a man that she met on a dating site. After having such a great time, they decided to go back to his place to Netflix and chill. He had in his mind that they were going to do more than chill and tried to rape her. She fought for her life and got away. All would have been fine if she had left it like that, but she did not.

She gathered a few of her male cousins and returned to his home. They broke in, beat, and raped him. The man didn't press charges. He probably assumed that the worse was over. It was not. She had him kidnapped and left him in the trunk of his own car for two days out in the woods. He got lucky when a hunter happened upon his car and freed him. This was the act that got her arrested and she served jail time as well.

Jade and Onyx are the only two precious stones that has never had a run in with the law, and she plans on keeping it that way. She misses her brother terribly and decides that she will call him for moral support once the divorce proceedings start. Her big brother always made her feel better and she knows that she will need him the most during this process.

Taji treks back downstairs to tell Jade that she's spoken with her lawyer friends and made them an appointment for next Tuesday. She finds Jade knocked out on the guest bed, leaving her be. Picking Bella up for snuggles, she hugs her and heads out the door. Taji told Jade that she had plans for tonight but that was a lie. The plan that she devised at the last minute was to search out Chosen and see where his mind was.

She knows she fucked up but has a serious issue with being able to admit when she's wrong. Even more of an issue when it came to apologizing. She tries calling him but doesn't get an answer so she decides to ride by his house.

Replaceable

I t's almost 8:00 P.M. and Chosen should be home by now. She debates on whether to seek him out or just let him come to her. *"What if he never does, though?"* That thought worries her, so she rolls the dice and pulls into his driveway. She sits in her car for a moment, trying to practice what she will say to him, but her mind goes blank. She doesn't do well with speaking from the heart, so she uses that thing that weighs eight pounds and sits on her neck and shoulders. Hoping that the right words will find her once she lays eyes on him. She hops out of the car, fixes her dress, and adds a couple of sprays of perfume before walking up to his door. She knocks and waits. No one answers. She knocks again, no response. This infuriates her, so she kicks his door and turns around to leave.

Getting back in her vehicle, she finds her phone and sends a text message to Chosen.

> Me: Listen, I know that you are upset with me. I should not have said the things that I said to you, and I should not have spoken to you like you were a child. That was wrong of me. Would you please call me when you get this message? I am sitting in front of your driveway.

Within seconds, her phone dings and Chosen has responded.

> Chosen: I am not at home now as you can see but we can talk Taji. Just not right now.

> Me: When? I want to see you ASAP.

> Chosen: See, there you go. Everything can't be how and when you want. I'll text you when I have time.

She desperately wants to snap but resists. Taji doesn't want to seem desperate, and she feels that is exactly how this exchange is making her appear. She doesn't like that feeling, so she decides not to respond at all.

"Shit, I'm muthafuckin' Taji, it ain't a nigga walking

this earth that's gonna make me wait like that. He must think that he's got the upper hand or something. Fuck him."

She backs out of the driveway and heads over to see Malcolm. She doesn't have to call and tell him that she's on the way. He's always happy to see her and waits on her hand and foot. Taji had Malcolm wrapped around her finger and she knew it. She was feeling a little down and nothing will lift a bitch's spirit like some good old fashioned head and pissing down a nigga's neck.

She arrives at Malcolm's place in just 20 short minutes, calling him as she pulls up to his gate. Knowing the code, she lets herself in. She parks and Malcolm meets her in the corridor looking all wide eyed.

"Umm, Taji, what's up? What are you doing here?"

"I've had a hell of a day, Malcolm, and I need your mouth."

"Well damn, Taji, tell me how you really feel."

"Now you know that I'm not the one to mince words, it has never been my style. Are you going to invite me up or am I supposed to stuff my pussy in your mouth in this corridor?"

"Forgive my manners, Taji, I'm not used to you calling me. I usually do the calling. I am a bit surprised is all," Malcolm admits.

"Don't be flattered," she says as she grabs Malcolm's

hand. "Press the elevator button and let's get this thing started." They enter the elevator, Malcolm sniffs her neck as he slides his hand under her dress. Her pussy welcomes him with open lips. He strokes her clit while licking her rock hard nipples. She shutters as he turns her around and drops to his knees to get a taste from the back.

Ding. The elevator bell rings.

"Damn Malcolm, that shit was just starting to feel good. Hurry up and get me into this apartment. My pussy is quaking for a sucking."

They breeze down the hallway, heading towards his condo. Malcolm opens the door and pushes Taji in.

"Hold on now, muthafucka... *I'm* the one that usually gives the orders. Don't be pushing on me," Taji gripes.

"Taji, shut up!" he commands, while pushing her against the wall and sliding her panties to the side. Dropping to his knees again, his tongue quickly finds her center. He teases then sucks her clit as he finger fucks her pussy. Taking his fingers out of Taji's snatch, he licks them one by one. While still against the wall, he rips her panties off. Lifting her entire body and sitting her on his shoulders, Taji's pussy is now directly in his face. He plunges his tongue deep inside and she whimpers from the pleasure.

Normally, she would be giving orders but this time, she doesn't have to. He must have wanted to taste the pussy just as bad as she wanted him to taste it. He devours her, lick by lick. Malcolm is talking shit the entire time because this time, he doesn't have to wonder if he is handling business. The moans and cries that Taji lets out is a definite sign that he is putting it down.

Grabbing her by the wrist, he walks her, still on his shoulders, from the wall to the couch. Laying her down gently while still licking and sucking her pussy to perfection. Taji's body trembles, and she feels herself giving in to the pleasure.

"Stop, Malcolm, stop. I'm not ready to cum yet."

"You may as well shut that shit up because I'm not stopping *shit*. This pussy and my tongue are best friends, and there's not shit that's going to separate me from my bestie right now. Not even you."

She looks down at him surprised because although he loves to tell her what to do, she rarely listens. This time, she shuts the fuck up and let it happen. Gleefully.

She cums at least five times before he lets her come up for air. She is tired, dehydrated, and ready for dick. Just not his. Malcolm's tongue was superb but the lower region of his body was just ok. Of the many times that they've hooked up, she's only let him inside her sugarwalls once. She was disappointed and pissed because he did not bring the thunder. Only a little sprinkle. According to her, that was his last time getting that chance.

She knew the night could not end properly unless she

was squatting over him. Being a human porta potty was the height of his night and since she was about ready to leave, she initiated it.

"Malcolm, let's go to the kitchen."

He jumps up in a hurry because he knows what that means. He helps her up and she can barely stand. Taji is as weak as water now. All that cumming has exhausted every piece of her energy. She shuffles over to the marble floors where Malcolm lies down and prepares to be soaked. What he got out of this she never understood but she didn't care. He paid good, licked good, and it cost her nothing to leave him with a parting gift. After the work that he has put in, she feels like he deserves it. Because she initiated it, he doesn't even have to compensate her for this session. This one is on her, just as piss is about to be on him.

"Are you ready, baby?" She queries while rolling her eyes and taking gulps of water.

"Yes, I am, please give it to me."

She squats over his chest and inches her way to his chin. She leans her body backwards, reaching for his dick. She finds his member and strokes him while he licks her swollen and tender clit for the last time tonight. He's going full speed with his tongue and adds two fingers for good measure. He knows just what she needs to get started and he gives it to her. He rams his fingers in and out her pussy while flicking his tongue so fast that it feels as if his mouth is vibrating. She leans back, relaxes, backs up away from his tongue, and let the golden showers flow.

Malcolm is beneath her, getting his whole life. She looks down and watches the way her piss drips from his neck and is amused to say the least. The floor slowly change colors to a pale yellow. She smiles as she looks down at his expression. If happiness had a face, it would be Malcolm. *Weird muthafucka*, she mutters under her breath.

"Yes, Taji, yes..." Malcolm moans, as he bucks and shudders. "Let me have it, baby. Give it all to me. Drench me, Taji. That feels so good," he moans.

"You like that, Malcolm? Let me see you gargle, baby."

"Yes, Taji, I love it. Your liquid honey is so warm, and it tastes so sweet. Girl, you know how to turn me the fuck on. Keep it coming for as long as you can. I need all that goodness."

When their human porta potty session ends, she does her normal routine, leaving him to clean up his mess while she takes a shower.

Once she bathes, she doesn't waste any time getting out of there. She collects her things and leaves immediately. Malcolm has served his purpose, and she no longer has a use for him tonight.

She leaves his condo waddling like a penguin. Her clit and pussy lips are swollen from all the friction but her head is clear. Malcolm put it on her ass. Getting in her car, she smiles and text him a simple message.

Me: I appreciate you.

Malcolm: Not more than I appreciate you. I don't want to take a shower because I want to keep you on me all night. Don't worry. I'm going to because I know that's nasty but girl... I love what you do to me. Drive home safely and text me when you get there

Me: Will do.

Taji is on cloud nine as she switches lanes, heading home. Once she arrives, she spots Teef's car in the driveway.

Oh, hell nawl. I know this son of a bitch didn't roll up to my crib. Taji says under her breath. To her surprise, he is sitting on her porch.

CHAPTER 8

Square Up

"Ummm, Teef. What the fuck are you doing here?"

"Don't call me that. My name is Reggie and I just pulled up, Taji. You know why I'm here. I'm here to get my wife and bring her home. This is stupid. She's mad about nothing."

"Nothing, you say. Giving my best friend Chlamydia is definitely *not* nothing, you nasty son of a bitch. Do you realize that you are putting her life at risk? Having sex with God knows who and *unprotected* at that. You should know better. If you were going to step out on your wife, the least your ass could have done was use protection. You men are so damn selfish and slow," she gripes as she walks past him and stands in front of her door.

"Teef, please get the fuck off my porch before I call the police on your ass. No one cares that you are the D.A... your ass can go to jail just like anyone else. Now go," Taji yells.

"No, bitch. I'm not going anywhere without my wife. The last thing that I need to do is leave her over here with your whorish ass. She'll come back being a slut just like you."

"Oh, so that's what it is, Mr. Sassy Pants? You don't want me to school her about niggas like you, huh? You're scared that she will get some sense if she sticks with me and you are right. My bitch is about to boss up and leave your ass. Trust and believe that."

"Oh, and if you thought that I would get offended by you calling me a whore, you are wrong. You've got to come harder than that to piss me off. Just in case you didn't know, a whore gets paid good to do what she does. A slut gives it away for free. I have never been nobody's slut. So it's *Mrs. Whore* to your sissy ass." Taji sucks her teeth as she slides her key in the door.

"What did you just say to me, bitch?" Teef questions as he puts his hands on Taji's shoulder and spins her around. "What did you say? Huh? Say it again, slut."

"I said get your sissy ass off my porch," Taji yells.

"Sissy, I'll show you a sissy, bitch," Teef murmurs and spits in Taji's face.

"I just know **the fuck you didn't!**" Taji yells as she begins knocking him upside his head. Holding his arms up and backing down the steps, Teef tries to protect his face, but Taji goes full throttle on his ass. Left hook, right hook, uppercut, all while kicking, screaming, and yelling. She's so loud that her neighbors have begun coming outside and standing on their porches to watch the show. Apparently, Jade hears the commotion and comes outside to find her best friend wearing her husband's ass out. Not in the way that he wants either. She is beating every part of his body that can be reached.

"Stopppp, Taji. Stop. What the hell is going on out here? Reggie, what in the fuck are you doing here?" Jade asks.

"Fuck what he's doing here, Jade. Your bitch ass husband just spit in my damn face. Ain't no telling what this muthafucka got. I'm going to kill his ass," Taji says as she tries to stomp him out. Teef is on the ground, trying to shield his body from the blows, but as soon as he covers up one part of his body, she hits another. Finally, a male neighbor of hers pulls her off him as Jade just stands there and looks on in horror.

"You sissy ass muthafucka. Fuck you and your bussy. Don't be mad at me because I know your truth. That you like *men* more than you like *your wife*. This is Atlanta, men liking men isn't anything new. Hey, live your truth. Just don't fuck over my friend while you do it."

"Please leave, Reggie, please!!!" Jade screams. "Why would you bring this kind of energy to Taji's house. You need to go. I don't want to talk to you or see you. Oh, and I want **a divorce**. Just so you know, I'll be filing the papers as soon as possible," Jade yells as Reggie gets up and stumbles to his car.

"Yeah, muthafucka, and don't *ever* bring your ass back to my house either. I'm going to press charges on you and I've got your bitch ass on camera. You didn't look up, did you? Smile, bitch. I will be making copies and turning over the evidence tomorrow. Have a nice night, you pussy," she says as she thanks the neighbor for intervening. "To all my neighbors that had to see that, I apologize but that nasty ass man just spit on me, and I blacked out," Taji yells.

"Come on, Taji, let's get you in the house and clean you up," Jade recommends.

"Bitch, I'm mad as hell. I had a great night, and he just had to bring his buck tooth ass over here and ruin it. I'd just gotten done almost getting my ovaries sucked out and then I come home to this shit. Now I have to take another shower. Fuck that, I'm going to take a bath with a teaspoon of bleach," she voices as she goes into her house and closes the door.

"Oh my goodness, Taji. I am so sorry that he would do such a thing to you. Or any woman. I swear, that man is changing right before my eyes. I don't know who he is anymore."

"What have I told you about apologizing for other people's actions. Once again, you did *nothing* wrong. Trust me, it's cool. I've got something for his ass, and I bet he won't see it coming."

"Oh Lord, what are you going to do, Taji? I'm just about afraid to ask. Are you really going to turn those tapes in tomorrow or were you just trying to scare him?"

"Girl, hell nawl, I'm not a snitch. I prefer to handle shit the street way. That nigga is the D.A. He will have that shit thrown out before the clock strikes twelve on tomorrow if it went that route. With people like that, I told you that you've got to move differently. I'm sure that he's hated by many. No one likes the D.A., so just keep that in mind. If someone fucks him up, they won't know who to look at, but it definitely won't be me or you."

"What does that mean? Are you going to tell me what you have up your sleeve?"

"Nope, what would the fun be in that? Plus, have you ever heard of the term *plausible deniability*? Your husband is the D.A., so I'm sure you have. You cannot tell what you do not know. Jade, I do need a favor from you though."

"Whatever it is, you've got it."

"Let me see your phone for just a minute. I'll give it right back, I promise."

Jade goes into the bedroom, comes back out, and hands Taji the phone. She presses a few buttons and gives it right back.

"Thank you," she utters as she walks up the stairs.

"Wait a minute, Taji, what did you just do?"

"Jade, you ask too many damn questions. I'm going to take me a nice hot bath. I need to get this battery acid off me and soak these pussy lips. They are sore."

"I thought you said that there wasn't going to be any hunching tonight."

"Who says that I hunched? I know that I sure didn't because that would be a lie. Anyway, mind your business and go back in your room and go to bed." Taji yells from upstairs. "Get some rest if you can because I plan on doing the same."

TAJI DRAWS a super-hot bath and puts a capful of bleach in her water just like she said she would. She slowly enters the tub, drops her shoulders, and relaxes. She thinks about Chosen and the words that she chose to say to him.

"Damn, he didn't even call me back either. It's ok though because just like I got his ass, I can get another."

She soaks, bathes, and hops out of the tub. Since she doesn't have anyone sleeping with her tonight, she opts for the comfortable moo-moo instead of the sexy lingerie. The events from today has Taji exhausted and she goes to sleep before her head hits the pillow.

CHAPTER 9

Thick and Thin

T aji wakes up the next morning and calls Diamond and Sapphire. She tells them what happened, and they are pissed. They know that their sister is too good for that kind of treatment, and they admit that they never liked him. They both felt that there was something off about Teef but they could never put their hands on it. They just thought that he was a tightwad because of his job but truthfully, that nigga is really awful down to the bone.

She purposefully leaves out the fact that Teef, may indeed, be cheating with a man. She leaves that up to Jade to tell. They will arrive in the upcoming weekend to surprise their baby sister. Taji tells them that she is setting up a full-on girls' day. She is going to plan a day with her personal manicurist, Amanda, her masseuse, Natasha, and her personal chef, Laquinta.

After the plans have been discussed, they agree that they would not tell Jade that Taji called them. She doesn't want Jade upset with her because she really is only trying to help. She treks downstairs to find Jade outside in the back yard with Bella. She's standing a little distance from the door, but Taji can hear her praying through the window. Slipping on her robe she goes outside and joins her. Jade is praying so hard in the spirit that she doesn't notice that Taji is standing beside her. Taji doesn't interrupt. She stands there still and lets Jade pray away.

Jade is startled when she opens her eyes to find Taji standing there with her arms raised in praise and her eyes are still closed. Taji lowers her hand, opens her eyes, and says, "I was just adding on to your prayer because there were some things that you left out, sis. Don't mind me. How are you feeling this morning? Are you ok, girl?"

"No, Taji, but I will be."

"Oh and we have an appointment next week with Roman. He is one of the best divorce attorneys in the state of Georgia and trust and believe that he is going to go to war for you."

"Good, I want to get this rolling and over as quickly as possible. I can't do this anymore. In fact, I've done it for too long. Anyway, I wanted to ask you, did you ever speak back to Chosen?"

"Ummm, about that, I tried reaching out to him but he told me that he would talk to me when he could find the time. He wouldn't even answer his phone for me. All I got was a text."

"Taji, are you going to start being honest with yourself? Like, we both know that you aren't going to get any better out here in these Atlanta streets. Atlanta may be full but there is definitely poop in the dating pool. You are in the streets like everyday. You know this already. Put your pride to the side and tell that man that you are sorry."

"Ok, then what? Are we supposed to just run off into the sunset after that and live happily ever after? Huh? Is that what you want me to say?"

"No, I want you to live in your truth like you told Reggie. Admit it, you love him. You are just afraid."

"Jade, I *am* living in my truth. I care about him a lot, but love is a bit too strong of a word for me. You need to slow down. You've got too much dip on your chip. Loving Chosen or any other man right now is not in my plan, remember?"

"Girl, fuck your plans." Jade blurts out and Taji clutches her invisible pearls.

"Ooh, Mrs. Thang, Teef really got you hot because you never drop those F bombs like that."

"Taji, be serious for a minute. Don't you know that life does not always go the way that we want? Have you ever heard the saying, 'God laughs when we make plans.' What do you think God is doing while you are running around thinking that you've got everything figured out? Taji, we are only getting older. Don't you want someone to do life with?"

"Jade, I'm not doing this. You know how I feel about these kinds of things, so I don't know why you are acting brand new. Like I told you before, none of these niggas are about to play in my face. That's all they do. You may as well hush because I don't want to hear this shit. I will apologize to Chosen but what I will not do is kiss his ass."

Taji calls Bella and the three of them enter back into the house.

"Oh, I sort of did a thing, but I don't want you to be mad at me, Jade, and I'm serious."

"Let me guess. You snuck out the house while I was asleep and went and slashed my husband's tires?"

"Girl, no, I would never do no childish shit like that. I'll leave that up to the kids and bitter baby mamas. When and if I get revenge, it would be on a bigger scale than that."

"Well, hopefully, you haven't done anything and won't do anything because his ass isn't worth it. Trust."

"That's not the point, Jade... that muthafucka spit in

my face and I'm supposed to just let that ride? I think the fuck not. That nigga has to know that he fucked with the wrong bitch. You know me better than most. You should know that there would be consequences for his actions. Why are you acting like we just met?"

"Because I was hoping that you would leave it alone. I am about to file for divorce. I don't need anything happening to him because people are going to automatically assume that I did it and I haven't done shit."

"Girl, stop with your paranoid ass. Now you know if I was to do something, I would cover my tracks. Nobody would know anything."

As Taji is schooling Jade on how to get away with murder, her phone rings. Chosen's name appears across the screen and Taji looks down, ignores the call, and continues talking.

Jade notices the name on the phone as well and stares at Taji and calls her a dumb ass without saying a word.

"Ummm, what? Why are you looking at me like that, Jade?"

"Because I'm trying to figure out why you didn't answer the phone. You know that you've been waiting to hear from him and there he goes on your line and you just ignored him. I swear, sometimes I don't understand you and the shit that you do."

"Jade, calm your muthafuckin' jets, please ma'am. I'm going to call him back. I just don't want to seem so eager. After all, he made me wait so his ass can wait, too. You seem really pressed about me talking to Chosen. Do you know something that I don't or do you have something that you want to tell me?"

"No, not at all, Taji. I just don't want you passing up the opportunity to make things right between you two. Like I said before, I like him for you. He matches your fly. He puts you in your place when need be but he is also gentle as a dove with you. I want you in a healthy relationship and I think that he's the one for that. Damn sure a better match than those other niggas that you have on your roster. Unless you want to go on another high speed chase," Jade giggles.

"Fuck you, Jade. I'm still not over that shit. Anyway, I'm going back up to my room to make my phone call in private. After that, I'm going to get dressed then I'll be back down in a little bit. We are going to go have brunch at your favorite spot, Breezy's Bistro, and for dinner, I've made reservations at Ruth Chris. That's what I was trying to tell you before I was rudely interrupted," Taji offers with a slick grin.

She then treks up the steps to her bedroom and closes the door. Sitting in the recliner chair with her head in her hands, she realizes that she's more nervous than antici-pated. *Taji, just make the damn phone call.* Nervously, she dials Chosen's number, and he answers on the first ring.

CHAPTER 10

Ultimatum

"Well, hi there, Mr. Chosen. How are you?"

"I've had better days but I'm maintaining," he responds. "What about you? How are you, Ms. Taji?"

"I'm ok. Look, you know I'm not the one to beat around the bush, so I just wanted to apologize to you and say that I'm sorry for speaking to you the way that I did. I'm also sorry for making you feel insignificant. Most of all, I'm truly sorry that you felt that I was wasting your time. That was never my intention. I have strong feelings for you, Chosen, but if I'm being honest, I am afraid that a quote-on-quote relationship between us will end up like all the others that I've seen. Null and void. That's why I never wanted to put a title on it. Titles make me nervous because what if I fail to meet your expectations or hell, even mine? I can't handle that pressure. I love the way we were. It just worked for us."

"No, Taji, it worked for *you*. Since we are being so upfront and honest, I guess it's my turn. When we first started seeing each other, I loved the fact that you lived so freely. On your own terms. Not a care in the world. After a while, I realized that you like that way of living because you lack accountability. You don't like deadlines, you don't like order, or even concrete plans. You are a *fly by the seat* kind of person. Now that's great when you are a teen or in your twenties, but for goodness sake, Taji. You are in your thirties."

"Chosen, what does me being in my thirties have to do with anything? Shit, I'm good over here."

"You've got to grow up, sweetheart. How long do you think that you will be able to run around here, siphoning money out these men, and making them move at your every whim? Not long, baby. Beauty and looks fade. You are going to have to have something else to offer."

"Chosen, in case you didn't know, I'm not nor have I ever lived my life by anyone else's rules but mine. I have lots to offer and I know what I want and what I don't want. I don't need you to tell me about me. I know my life. I'm the one living it. Just because I don't want to rush to have a family and set up house doesn't mean that I'm just out here being reckless the way that you think I am. I mean yeah, I do what I do but I am careful in who I deal with. My looks may fade but this personality and swag will always be here. Hell, that's what got you, isn't it? Furthermore, I don't appreciate you trying to down talk me, Chosen. That shit isn't cool. I have not said one bad thing about you."

"I'm not down talking you, love. You are missing the point. The point is that I am here and willing to accept you just as you are. Flaws and all and you treat me like I'm *disposable*. I'm not and just because you can't see my worth, doesn't mean that it's not there."

"I've never thought that you were disposable. What I did think was that you were on board for all of this without conditions. You knew that I didn't want to settle down. You knew that I didn't want kids anytime soon. We were supposed to be chillin'. When I'm with you, Chosen, I'm with you. When I'm not, I'm not. I thought that was clear and cool with you. I need to know what changed?"

"Me, Taji. **Me.** I've changed. I was hoping that we would grow together but you've stayed idle. Doing the same shit day after day. I'm not doing that. Like I said in that text that I sent you, I want a family, a sense of normalcy. Period. I'm a man, I want to leave a legacy. I need a woman that is ok with one man and one man only. I'm not sharing my wife with anyone, ya dig."

"If you are willing to work on that with me then we can move forward. If you aren't, then this will be the last time that you hear from me. I have to move on with my life and find someone that wants the same things that I do. I'll give you 5 days to make up your mind. Please don't contact me again until that time is up. Goodbye, Taji," Chosen whispers as he hangs up the phone.

Taji looks down at her cell phone in disbelief, but she listened intently at what Chosen said. She heard him loud and clear but doesn't feel like giving her an ultimatum is the way to go.

"This negro knows that I hate being told what to do. Like if I were about to do it, now I'm not because who in the fuck does he think he is?"

Whatever. I don't have time for this shit.

Taji puts her phone on the charger and heads into her closet to pick out her ensemble. She chooses a sexy little cocktail dress, a pair of nude pumps, and an array of diamonds: necklaces, earrings, and bracelets from her previous lovers. She meticulously chooses what to wear because you never know who you may run into while you are out. She bathes and jumps out of the shower and dries off.

She sits in front of her vanity to style her hair and beat her face to perfection. She even adds a red lip because she feels spicy. After she's all put together, she saunters downstairs to find Jade sitting on the couch crying yet again.

"What's wrong, honey dip? Did you get a call from Teef or something?"

"No, my sisters called me and told me that they miss me and that they wanted to see me. They said that they would be here this weekend. Taji, how am I going to explain to them what I am going through? When I pick them up from the airport and don't bring them to my house, they are going to know that something is wrong. I swear that I don't want them in my business. What am I supposed to say?"

"Jade, let me handle it. You don't have to say anything. I will go get them and bring them back over here. You just tell them that since both of them are coming, we are going to do like old times and have a sleepover at my house. How long will they be here?"

"Just the weekend I believe. I know they have work so it can't be for that long."

"Exactly, so you will tell them that I have planned a weekend full of activities at my house. First, we will start with pedicures, a massage, and I will have my chef come and whip us up a good old-fashioned seafood spread. How does that sound?"

"Taji, you would do all that for me?"

"You are my best friend, my rock. I would do anything,

and I mean *anything,* for you," Taji says as she hugs Jade and smiles awkwardly as they embrace.

Taji hated to play dumb like she didn't know what was going on. She didn't want to lie to her friend but she really would do anything for Jade. Thus, the reason that she called her sisters this morning. I mean, Jade wasn't going to do it, and she needs love, support, and affection right now. Oh, and if they kick that nigga's ass in the process, that will be ok with Taji as well.

"Now, stop that damn crying and hurry up and get dressed. I thought that I would be the one that's late but it's you. According to Chosen, I don't do shit right. I never make plans and if I do, apparently I'm always late. Guess I should call him and let him know that I was on time today," Taji gripes in a facetious tone.

"Girl, when did he say that? Tell me everything that he said," Jade utters as she attempts to sit back on the couch to sip the tea.

"Nope, I'll tell your ass over brunch," Taji offers as she grabs her elbow and raises her back up. "Girl, I'm hungry and you are over here playing around while I'm starving. I'll be in the car waiting," Taji murmurs as she grabs her things and heads out the door.

They arrive at the bistro and can't help but to notice that it's packed. The line is down the street and appears to be moving at a snail's pace.

"Jade, I know that you love this place but I am not about to wait in line for no damn chicken and waffles. We can just go to the Waffle House for all that. I'm not trying to be difficult but do you see these heels? These are *go in and find your seat* heels. Not stand in a line for 2 hours waiting on waffles and to take pictures in front of the grass wall heels."

"I know. I never wait in line. I'm good friends with the owner. Let me just make a phone call and I'm sure that he will get us in asap."

"Ok then, Ms. Pull Those Strings. I know that's right. *Use what you've got to get what you want,*" Taji recites. They look at each other and burst out laughing. *Player's Club* was one of their favorite movies and they were known for quoting it at any point and time of the day.

"Sssshhhhh, Taji, with your goofy ass. I'm trying to use my sexy voice and I can't do that if I'm laughing," Jade confesses as she dials the number and puts the phone to her ear.

"Umm... yes, hi. Is this Soiree? Hi, Soiree, this is Jade. We were trying to get into your lovely establishment, but we noticed that the line is down the street. Would you happen to have room in there for two beautiful ladies or shall we venture off to the Waffle House?" Jade giggles in a sexy tone.

"Ok, well thank you. I'll meet you at the back entrance," she voices as she disconnects the phone call.

"Girl, who in the hell is a Soiree?" Taji gabs.

"Oh, nobody special. He's just a friend of mine. I usually come in here with a few co-workers and at times we would chat it up. He always told me that anytime I wanted to dine, just give him a ring and he would get me in. Now, I never wait in line."

"I see," Taji nods, grabbing her purse from the backseat and hopping out the BMW.

CHAPTER 11

Daddy's Girl

They trek to the back of the restaurant and is let right in by a fine ass Sudanese brother whose skin resembled 97% dark cocoa. He is one of the most beautiful chocolate men that Taji's ever seen and that says a lot. He is dressed to the nines. All designer. A tailored to perfection white Thom Browne button-down shirt, Givenchy slacks, and a pair of Christian Louboutin Dandelion loafers. A custom Rolex watch, no jewelry on the neck, but a simple Just en clou Cartier bracelet adorns his wrist.

He grabs Jade's hand and walks her right up to a table and seats them both. He bends down and kisses her gently on the cheek, smiling and telling them that their waitress will be right with them.

"Ma'am, that didn't look like a friendly kiss to me. Did

you see how that man was looking at you? There has got to be more to him than what you are telling me because let me find out."

"Seriously, Taji, we've only spoken in here. Never outside this restaurant. I'm not sure but I think that he has a wife."

"Does he know that? Because I damn sure wouldn't want my husband slobbing all over another woman."

"Hey, I'm just here to eat. Nothing more. I don't know what he's got going on in his mind and I do not care. It has nothing to do with me."

"Well, what else do you know about him? He seems very well put together and this place is nice as hell. Is this his only spot?"

"No, Taji, we aren't doing that today."

"Doing what? I just asked a question. What do you think that I'm doing?"

"I didn't just meet you. You are vetting that man. Trying to see if he will become a member of your roster aren't you?"

"Wrong, the roster is closed for now. I'm not recruiting right now but if I was, he would definitely be up next. I honestly was asking for you. Not me."

"Well, you can save those questions. I'm not interested. I'm not even divorced yet and you are already trying to pawn me off to someone else. Can I go and heal first?" Jade requests as she picks up the menu from the table.

"Well damn. Bite my head off then. I hope you plan on getting a few mimosas as well because you damn sure need a drink or something. Calm down, Jade. No one is trying to make you do anything that you don't wanna do."

"I'm sorry, Taji, I shouldn't have snap like that. I know that you have my best interest at heart and you just want to see me happy. I want the same for you. Now let's go ahead and order because I think that I'm just hangry," they cackle.

After they finish stuffing their faces, Soirée comes over to the table and tells them not to worry, that their bill has been taken care of.

Jade gives him a hug and Taji leaves a huge tip for the waitress. As they move towards the back entrance, Soirée stops Jade and asks if he can have a moment with her. She obliges and Taji continues out the door, heading to the car.

While sitting in the car and waiting for Jade to come out, Taji scrolls through the pictures of her and Chosen and can't help but to think of the good times that they shared. In all reality, she could see herself spending the rest of her life with him. The one and only thing holding her back is *fear*. Fear of trusting a man in any capacity. That just has never worked out well for her. She pushes Chosen to the back of her mind and turns the radio on as an escape. Johnnie Taylor's *Running Out of Lies*, starts blasting through the speakers. A song that she heard 100 or more times as a child. Her father used to play it often while she was growing up and as she listens to the words, she transcends to an earlier time in her life.

SHE STARTS THINKING about the only man that she ever truly loved. Her father. She was a daddy's girl from the very beginning and in her eyes, her father could do no wrong. Taji grew up in a two-parent household, full of love, joy, and the freedom of expression. Through innocent eyes, her parents appeared to be the perfect couple, throwing parties and entertaining were their specialties. Her mother was a stay-at-home mom and her father was a street pharmacist with a reputation that preceded him. His birth name was Indigo. Taji's mother told her that the name fit him perfectly because he was dark like the sky at twilight and a rare commodity. The two seemed to get along famously. That was until the day her father's side chick knocked on the door and the world as she knew it crumbled.

Taji remembers waking up to the sounds of glass breaking and bodies crashing into the wall. Running out of her room to see what the commotion was, Taji was thrown right in the middle. Her father urged her to come stand by him and her mother warned her to get away from him. She didn't know which way to turn so she turned back and went into her bedroom closet to escape the chaos. Scared and confused, she stayed there until everything went back to normal but things never did go back to normal. Once the house grew quiet, Taji emerged from the closet to find her mother weeping on the kitchen floor.

Realizing that her daughter had entered into the kitchen, her mother jumped up, grabbed Taji, squeezed her tight, wiped her tears, pushed her vulnerability to the side, and had a heart to heart with her daughter.

"Baby girl, I'm sorry that you had to see that, but there are some things that I have to explain to you. I know that you are only nine and that this is a lot for someone your age, but I wouldn't be a good mother to you if I didn't tell you the truth."

"Your dad is gone and I don't know if he's ever going to come back. I'm telling you this because I don't want you waiting for him just in case he doesn't."

"What do you mean that he isn't coming back? Mama, what is going on and who was that lady that knocked on the door?"

"Baby, your daddy and I are no longer together as of today and that woman was his girlfriend."

"Girlfriend, Mama? I don't understand. I thought that

you were his wife. How can Daddy have a girlfriend and a wife?"

"You know, little girl, that's a great question. One that I don't have an answer to, but don't you worry about anything. I know what my job is and that is to take care of you and make sure that you have everything that you need."

And that was exactly what her mother did. Her father left that day and never returned. He never called, came by, sent any money, or anything. A few years later, someone called her mother and said that he was missing but no one truly knew where he went.

The day that Taji's father walked out of hers and her mother's life was the day that she stopped trusting men. I mean how could she? He left them with *nothing*. Her mother worked job after job to provide. Eventually, she went back to school and received a nursing degree that provided a surefire way of taking care of her daughter, but it wasn't easy, and Taji saw and recognized that. She always commended her mother because she never mumbled a bad word about her father, but she didn't have to. The hurt that she watched her mother endure after he left burned a hole through her heart and her mother's heart as well. Taji doesn't know if her father is the reason or not but her mother, Jordan, remains single til' this day.

Taji's father was the first man to ever love her, and he

was also the first man to ever break her heart. Her distrust for men was deeply rooted in something that she herself couldn't understand or fix.

SHE IS SNAPPED back to reality when Jade opens the car door and plops down.

"Well damn bitch, that took forever. I thought that I was going to have to come back in there and get your ass. That man didn't have you hemmed up in the freezer, did he?" Taji queries.

"No, fool. He just wanted to discuss something personal with me."

"Please don't tell me that it is what I think it is. Please," Taji utters with a mischievous grin.

"No, Taji, he didn't ask if Reggie was gay. It was about his niece's case. He was wondering if there were any new discoveries, and it pained me to tell him no."

"Oh ok. I thought that you all were in there getting freaky deaky. Now that we are full as ticks, what's next, Jade? Today is your day so what do you want to do?"

"I need to go home and pick up some new clothes. Reggie is at work now so at least I won't have to see him, but I think I'll wait until after my sisters leave."

"You should wait until this weekend when your sisters

are here. That way, you will have backup and won't have to worry about him getting rowdy with you. He wouldn't dare do that shit with Sapphire and Diamond around. He knows better," Taji laughs.

"Now Taji, you know damn well that I'm not going to take them over there. Anyway, I'm sleepy and I've got the itis. I know you do, too, so why don't we go and take a nap?"

"We can do that, but I need to stop at Sephora and pick up a few things. Are you ok with that or do you want me to drop you off first?"

"Please, if you don't mind. Girl, I've got to use the bathroom, and you know that I don't just poop anywhere. I think that the syrup got me."

"Girl, I don't need any details."

Taji drops Jade back off at the house and proceeds to Sephora.

CHAPTER 12

Intruder Alert

Before she puts her car in park, she receives a phone call from Jade.

"Taji, you need to come back home now. Somebody has been in the house, and I'm scared."

"Say less. I'm on the way."

Taji backs out of her parking space and races home to find Jade outside on the porch trembling. Taji goes back to the car to the glove box to retrieve her Ruger. Just to be on the safe side.

"Jade, go sit in my car. I'm going to go through the house and see what kind of damage has been done or if they are stupid enough to still be in there."

"Wait, I can tell you. The only thing that has been messed with is the room that I am staying in. The drawers have been gone through, as well as the bathroom and closet. The few little clothes that I have are all over the place. Nothing is missing. Just rummaged through. Girl, I know ain't nobody did this shit but Reggie. It has to be because they didn't bother your shit at all, and you are the one with the valuables. He needs to leave me the fuck alone."

"Taji, I know that you don't want to get the police involved, but don't you think that we should call them now? Like, this shit is ridiculous."

"Call them for what? It's not like we don't know who did this shit. Don't worry, Jade. We are gonna handle it. Plus, if you really wanna be certain, just give me a few. I'll go back there and check the footage from the cameras. I bet we will see Teef's ass on there."

"Taji, he's too smart for that. He would have hired someone and sent them over here. He wouldn't have done it himself. He's too scary and doesn't like to have his name attached to anything scandalous."

"Well, he might want to start with not cheating on his wife with men and spitting on her best friend. That would make a hell of a good start. I will never understand how men have the unmitigated gall to do half of the shit that they do and then acts surprised when they get left. Like, did you not even consider that your wife leaving you was a possibility? I told you that they asses be slow. Anyway, you start to clean this shit up and I'm going to go check the cameras."

Jade was correct. Teef isn't on the cameras, but some random nigga is. Taji is super pissed and feels violated because someone has been in her home and there is no telling if they bugged the place. She sits to think about who she can call to come over and sweep the place for bugs and one face pops into her mind, Ajani. Ajani happens to be the guy that installed the cameras from the beginning. He would know where to start so she gives him a ring and he offers to swing by after work. As their phone call concludes, Chosen's face appears in Taji's mind.

She wants to call him and let him know all the things that have happened since his departure, but he told her that he didn't want to hear from her until her waiting period was over. Following his orders, she puts her phone back on the charger while shrugging her shoulders. Taji goes back into the common area and Jade is a mess. Crying as she sweeps and cleans up the broken glass.

"Jade, I promise you that everything will be ok. There is no need to cry. Teef is going to get his, one way or the other. Now, like I told you earlier, we aren't going to call the police. We are going to handle him ourselves. Well, I take that back. *I'm* going to have it handled. I only need one thing from you."

"And what is that?" Jade responds.

"I need the security code to your home, and I don't want you to tell it to me. I want you to write it down on a sheet of paper and leave it on my nightstand. Also, I want you not to ask me any questions. No matter what you hear out in these streets. Don't ask me shit. Ok?"

"At this point, I'll do whatever you say. I just want this shit to be over and it hasn't even started. Are you sure that this Roman guy is solid?"

"Girl, don't insult me. Now you know I don't deal with anything but the best and that is in any area of my life."

"I sure hope so, Taji. I don't know how much of this shit I can take. I wish that I could go and buy a house right damn now and move in it, but I know that his trifling ass would fight me for it in the divorce. If I never saw him again in life, it would be too soon. You know, Taji, I still can't believe that he would do this to me. To us. I truly thought that we had something great, but I was wrong."

"Taji, why? Why wasn't I good enough? Am I not alluring or sexy enough? Did I not cater to him enough? Did I work too much? Did I not keep myself up? I have gained about 20 pounds, but I think that I still look good. Maybe I'm just too big for him now. Be honest. Am I a mess? Am I ugly or something?"

"Jade, don't ask me no stupid shit like that. You know that you are beautiful. Gorgeous even and I'm not just saying that because you are my best friend. Bitch, friend or not... if you were ugly, I would say that. You are not and I refuse to let you sit here and blame yourself for that nigga's actions. You are always doing that and I am always fussing at you about it. Stop it. I hate self-deprecation."

"Taji, I'm just trying to understand. I did *everything* that a wife is supposed to do. How could he just throw caution to the wind like that? Fucking people raw. That's just nasty and I could never. I can't mean shit to him if he could do me like this. *Me*, the woman that has been with him from the very beginning. When his ass used to wear high waters and those too little shirts. Not to mention those damn coke bottle glasses and teeth. He was a mess. No one was checking for him. All the girls thought that he was a goofy. In reality, he was, but I saw past all of that. I saw deeper and he's nothing like the person that I married. Now, his ass is insufferable."

"How about we don't talk about him anymore today unless we have to? I mean not one mumbling word about Teef. Especially not until we make sure that his ass didn't leave any bugs around. Let's clean up and get ready for tonight."

"Taji, do you think that I should hire somebody to watch this place?"

"Like who, the police? If that's who you have in mind, then hell no. That's the last thing that I want."

"Taji, why do you hate the police so bad? You don't have any warrants and you are a law abiding citizen. I just don't see why you are bothered by them so much."

"You want to know why for real? I'm going to tell you. Two summers ago, I went out on a date with a police officer, and it didn't go well. You know that I am a straight shooter, so I told him that I wasn't interested in a second date because we lived two different lifestyles. I just couldn't see how it would work. The brother was cheap and obnoxious."

"I thought that that was the end of it but he kept calling me. So, like any bad bitch like myself would do, I blocked him. He still would not leave me alone. He started calling from different numbers. He was riding by my house and all kinds of creepy shit. Then, he told me that he could have me touched any time that he wanted to and I believed him. If we call the police, there is a chance that he could show up and that is the last thing that I want. I need his creep ass as far away from me as possible. Him and his little police friends."

"Jade, from my experience, police officers are some of the most controlling men that I have encountered. They are bossy and be on power trips and I'm not with none of that shit. Now do you understand?"

"Yes, I do. Damn, Taji. You have been through the ringer with these men. I see why you are scared to make that jump from being single to a relationship. I get it now."

"Jade, that's just one of the reasons. There are so many more but there isn't enough time in this day. Plus, I don't want you talking about your issues with Teef, so I'm not about to talk about my issues with these niggas. After Ajani gets here and leaves, so are we. We are going to find something to do that doesn't consist of you sitting here sulking. Your sisters will be here in a couple of days. You've got to put your happy face on. You know those bitches can sniff out when someone is playing on their tops. You better have your shit together, Jade."

"Oh, I plan on it. I'm keeping them out my business by any means necessary."

"Good, are you excited to see them?"

"I am, but I'm nervous at the same time. I'm going to try not to drink too much because you know when I drink, it's hard for me to watch my words. They will know it all before the night ends if I have too many shots of Casamigos."

"It may not be a bad thing that they know something. Those girls love you. Don't you think you need to be around people that have your back? Well other than me, of course."

"I do and I'm glad that they are coming, but I just

don't want them getting into any shit. It's like trouble finds them."

"Trust me, I understand that all too well. Now that you've got this room all spic and span, why don't you go back in there and take that nap that you were talking about after we left the restaurant. I will stay up and make sure that nothing happens."

"I'm going to do just that, Taji. I'm still tired and I'm still full. Just wake me up when your camera guy gets here."

"I will. Have a nice nap, sis."

Jade returns to her bedroom to take her nap. Taji treks outback with Bella to get a little fresh air and figure out what her next move will be. The events of today have provided her with the opportunity to completely ignore Chosen's words, but they were never far from her mind. Taji isn't stupid. She realizes what is on the line and truly doesn't want to lose him. On the other side of things, she doesn't feel as if she should be made to make a choice.

The decision to settle down with someone should be organic. Not forced or pressured. History has shown Taji that things never end up well when they are forced.

CHAPTER 13

The Reason

Taji was 16 when her mom's best friend's nephew, Marcus, came to stay for the summer. An 18-year-old Boston native with a serious chip on his shoulder. Although she was practically infatuated with Marcus, he didn't have a clue because she always had a mean poker face. She treated him just like any other boy on her block, like nothing special. Marcus was visiting his aunt for the summer and he and Taji became fast friends. Since her mother and his aunt were besties, they practically did everything together. Taji's mom, Jordan, and Marcus's aunt, Sonia, would frequent the club each weekend and return home around 3 AM.

This had been their routine for many years, and they were able to keep that up because in their eyes, the children were old enough to take care of themselves. Which they were. Taji was an only child and had been looking after herself for years. Jordan worked a full-time job, sometimes two, just to make ends meet and Sonia did the same. Sonia didn't have any children, but she considered Marcus to be the next best thing. She helped raise him when her younger sister had him at a young age. She spoiled him rotten. He would often throw tantrums when he didn't get his way, and this made Marcus unbearable to be around at times.

They spent many nights together with no major incidents, but this night was different. The adults were playing blues and getting ready to step out. Everyone was singing and dancing and just having a great time. Sonia cooked fried chicken, green beans, and macaroni and cheese so that Marcus and Taji would have something to eat while they were away.

As usual, Marcus and Taji would watch horror movies until the adults came back from the club. The horror film *Paranormal Activity* had just come out on DVD and Marcus was excited to watch it. Horror movies were his favorite. Taji only watched them because she was fond of him and at that age, peer pressure wins nine out of 10 times.

When things got a little too scary for her, she decided to leave him up and head to bed. That night, Marcus decided that he did not want to watch the movie alone and entered Taji's room. He wanted her to come back into the living room and finish the movie with him, which she declined. She explained that she was tired and that they could watch it another night.

Marcus wouldn't take *no* for an answer and proceeded to yank Taji from her bed. She pushed him away and this angered him. Marcus came after Taji with full force, knocking her against the wall. Hitting her head and falling unconscious, Taji woke up to Marcus on top of her, raping her mercilessly. Once she came to, she fought and fought to get him off her. Sadly, she was no match for the 6 foot 2 inches, 215 pound 18-year-old.

That night, Marcus took her virginity and her innocence and Taji didn't say a word. That was until she missed a couple of periods. Her mother noticed when she realized that she hadn't purchased any pads or tampons for Taji in months. Her mother paid close attention to those kinds of things and began to question her daughter over and over. Taji refused to tell what had happened to her because in her mind, it was her fault. She thought that she would be blamed for what happened so she kept quiet. She kept that secret until those two lines popped up on that Dollar Tree pregnancy test that her mother brought home and forced her to take.

A tearful Taji began to recount the events that took place that night and her mother wept. She cried harder than she'd ever seen her mother cry before. Feeling like she failed her daughter, she apologized profusely to Taji and promised that Marcus would pay for what he did. Her mother kept her promise.

First she called the police then she called Sonia over and told her what happened. When Sonia said to her that her nephew wouldn't do such a thing and that Taji must be lying, Jordan dived on top of Sonia and whooped her ass until the police arrived. Marcus was supposed to leave and head back to Boston in a week, in order to prepare for his new job, but he never made it. Taji's mother pressed charges and Marcus was promptly arrested and charged with assault and 1st degree rape. He was sentenced to 12 years. As for the baby, Taji always had plans on going off to college and wasn't about to let anything stop her. She asked her mother for an abortion and her mother accommodated her request.

Taji never looked back and decided that she would never fall victim and be at another man's mercy. She vowed that she would live her life to the fullest. Living and moving on her own terms. In her mind, she would be the *head bitch in charge*. She also never had any kind of counseling for what she went through. Instead, she carries that hurt everywhere she goes and allows her hurt to fuel her distrust for men.

Taji decides that she's done enough thinking for today and it was time to have a little fun. Too much seriousness always puts her in a bad headspace and she isn't very rational when this happens. She wants to finish her trip to Sephora but she knows that Jade will be uncomfortable if she's left alone. Especially after coming home to a room completely ransacked by a total stranger so she scoops Bella up and they return into the house.

She checks the clock and impatiently waits for Ajani to arrive. Getting off in less than 20 minutes, he should arrive in no time.

The doorbell rings and Taji tells him through the door-bell camera that he may enter.

"Jade," Taji yells. "Ajani is here. Come out the room so that he can start his sweep in there."

"Hello, Ajani, welcome... come on in," she says as she swings the door open.

Ajani sees Taji again and starts to thirst immediately. Just as he did the first time he saw her. She smiles and watches him watch her as she sashays around the living room. She knows the power that she holds over men and uses it to her advantage every chance that she gets.

"Hey, Taji," Ajani responds, blushing like a school girl. "You gave me a brief explanation about what happened but I was kind of in the middle of something and couldn't pay attention the way that I needed to. Would you mind telling me what happened."

As he is talking, Jade enters into the living room and Ajani's eyes shift towards her.

"Well, hello, Ma'am. I'm Ajani. I work for Kinsley Communications and Technologies and I am here to do a total sweep of the house."

"Oh, excuse my manners. Ajani, this is my best friend, Jade. She's going to be staying here with me for a while. I want to make sure that we are secured in every way possible. We think that her soon to be ex-husband had someone come in here while we were gone earlier today. They didn't seem to take anything so that made me believe that they planted something. I need you to sweep every inch of this house to make sure that there are no bugs or any other devices that you didn't install. Do you remember where you put everything last time?"

"I sure do and I will get right to it," Ajani assures.

"Good, we will be outback if you need us. Please be thorough."

"No worries, Taji. I will. I promise.

Taji and Jade step out back on the deck to let Ajani do his thing.

"Jade, I figured out what we could do once he leaves. We can go ahead and go back to Sephora and then after that, we'll do a little shopping. You said that you needed clothes and it is about time that I help you upgrade that wardrobe of yours."

"What do you mean help me upgrade? Are you trying to say that my clothes are terrible?"

"Nope, but you could use a little help in the styling department. Your clothes aren't terrible at all. I just want to help you look and feel better and nothing makes a woman feel like a woman more than shopping. At least for me. The clothes that you brought over aren't Ruth Chris ready and I want you to be on point tonight."

"I'm down with that. It sounds fun actually. I can't remember the last time that I went to the mall and dropped a bag on myself."

"Exactly and it is long overdue. Between Teef and those dead people, you need a break. It's time to let that pretty hair down and show off that big old donkey that you are carrying. You've got a perfect shape, Jade. Bitches in Atlanta pay great money to look the way that you do and you got it naturally. It's nothing wrong with showing it off sometimes. I know you aren't looking for anyone, but a little male attention won't hurt either. I'm not saying that you have to talk to them, but trust, men ogling over your goodies will make you feel like the baddest bitch in the land."

"Taji, I'm not checking for these men, and they don't

need to be checking for me. I'm trying to get through dealing with the hurt from my husband and the shit that he did to me. Then figure out this divorce thing and settlement, not to mention splitting all of our assets. It's just a lot. I'm tired even thinking about it."

"And you will overcome everything and come out victorious. I'm sure of it."

CHAPTER 14

Your Love Awaits

"Jade, I want to tell you something that I've never shared with anyone else. My mother was a good woman, just like yourself. She took care of home, me, and my father. There wasn't anything that she wouldn't do for us. My father was in the streets and you know what comes with being in the streets. Drama and chaos."

"My life was damn near a Disney movie until it wasn't. Once all was said and done and the smoke cleared, it was just my mother and I, and that is the way that it remained until I went off to college. He hurt her so bad that she never loved again. That's why when we were in college, I made it my business to go home as often as I could. Without me, my mother was by herself and I hated that for her. My mom is beautiful and could've had any man that she wanted, but she wanted my father and he wanted the streets."

"A long time ago, when I was about 13, I asked her why she never chose to date again and she said that it just wasn't worth it. She told me that she never wanted to bring another man around because she didn't trust men with me. I hated that she felt this way because I didn't want my mom to be alone. She deserved a good man because she was a good woman."

"I didn't sweat it too much because I just knew that when I went off for college, that my mother would live her best life. That was my hope for her, but as far as I know, she hasn't. She gets up in the morning and goes to the hospital. She works her 8 to 12 hours and goes straight home just like you did."

"Taji, why are you telling me this?"

"Because I don't want you to end up like my mother. I don't want you to let what one man did to you, stop you from loving. From living."

"I know that there is someone out there that's perfect for you. Understandably you're not interested right now, but I just don't want it to stray too far from your mind. Teef was never good enough for you. I saw that from the day that you brought him to our dorm room. I didn't say anything because I'm not a hater and I honestly thought that you would see it over time but you never did."

"Taji, I know damn well you aren't over here, trying to school me about loving somebody when you have a man that kisses the ground that your ass walks on. Yet, I don't see you ready to jump the broom. You don't take that man seriously at all. Now, I love you like a sister, but don't try to check me about some shit that you won't even do yourself."

"Yeah, but we're not talking about me."

"You may not be talking about you, but I am. You can find a way to fix everything wrong in everyone else's life but what about fixing the shit in yours?"

"Do you not think that you are worthy of the same thing, Taji? Just like me, you deserve love, too."

"The difference is, I don't want it."

"What do you mean you don't want it? Are you saying that you *never* want to be in love?"

"Yes, that's what I'm saying."

"Are you serious right now? You can't be sitting in my face telling me that my great love awaits and you don't even believe in love."

"I don't believe in love for *myself*, but I believe in it for you."

"Taji, I want you to know that you sound crazy as hell. Is it that you don't think that you are worthy?"

"Quite contrarily, it's the other way around. See, I look at it like this. My heart is precious. Too precious to even risk it being broken again. Men constantly lie, cheat, and disappoint. I'm not having that shit and the way that my mind is set up, crashing out because you played in my face is imminent. I don't want to go to jail."

"So are you saying that you don't love because you are scared that if you give your all to someone and they don't reciprocate, that you might crash out?"

"There isn't *any might* in it. I **will.** You can only get hurt if you care. I make it my business *not* to care."

"Well, Taji, I'm just gonna tell you because I'm not scared of you," Jade giggles. "That stupid as hell and sad."

"Call it what you want. I call it self-preservation."

Hearing the back door open, Ajani interrupts their banter to let Taji know that he's done. He found nine recording devices throughout the house and she is livid. Ajani walks them around to show them exactly where each device was placed.

Most of them were in the common areas but there was one in Taji's room, the room that Jade sleeps in, and the other guest rooms. Ajani advises that he did a thorough sweep, even outside to make sure that there weren't any other cameras that he didn't install. He didn't find any cameras, but that doesn't make them feel any better.

Taji feels violated and knows that this shit has to stop now.

"Well, thank you so much, Ajani for your services. Just send me your invoice and I'll take care of it."

Jade interrupts, "No, you can send that invoice to my email and I'll take care of it. All of this is my fault, and I won't sit here and let you pay for anything else, Taji."

"Well, I will let you two ladies sort that out. Taji, you have my number just in case you need anything else."

"I do and I won't hesitate to use it," she winks.

Ajani smiles and states, "I sure hope that you don't. You need to use it so we can set up a day that I can take you out."

"Trust me, Ajani. You don't want any parts of me. I would ruin your life."

"Come on, Taji. You can't be that bad."

"Yes, she can," Jade interrupts. "Once again, thank you so much for your services and I'll be sending the payment as soon as you send the invoice to me. Have a great day, Mr. Ajani, and it was nice to meet you."

"You ladies enjoy the rest of your day," he says as he leaves out the front door.

"Well damn, bitch, you didn't have to make the man think that I was the damn grim reaper," Taji says.

"I can't believe this shit. This muthafucka really came up in my house and planted some damn bugs. Who the fuck does he thinks that he is? Bitch, Teef's ass has got to go."

"I know, Taji. I'm so sorry about all of this. I'm going to call him now and let him know that we found the little friends that he left behind."

"Girl, that shit ain't going to do any good. You know his beaver mouth ass is just going to deny it. He will never admit to it."

"You're right, Taji. He won't but I'm still calling because I need to let him know that I am not going down without a fight. Like, what would make him think that any of this shit is ok?"

"Well, I thought that it was obvious by now that he doesn't think at all. How he ever became the District Attorney is beyond me."

Jade treks into her room to retrieve her phone to call Reggie and give him a piece of her mind.

CHAPTER 15

Prey

"Ummm, Reggie. I just want you to know that I know that you had someone come into Taji's house and had the house bugged but all those fuckers are gone. You really be thinking that you are smarter than everyone else, don't you?"

"Jade, I don't know what the hell you are talking about. I haven't been to that crazy bitch's house since the other night."

"Sure you haven't. You will tell me anything. I know it was you because who else would do such a thing. Nobody else even has a reason."

"Probably one of the niggas that Taji fucks with. She's a whore. Whores are always pissing people off. She probably robbed somebody with her ghetto ass."

Taji hears her name being said over the phone and goes off.

"Listen here, Boochie cat. Keep my muthafuckin' name out of your nasty ass yuck mouth. I have nothing to do with this conversation. You are always on my dick, which isn't *unusual* for you, but this isn't what you want over here. So please find you something safe to do and leave me out of it."

"What the fuck do you mean that it isn't unusual for me? Just what in the hell are you trying to insinuate?"

"You know what, Teef. I'm not having this conversation. Your soon to be ex-wife is talking to you. Not me," Taji mutters as she walks into the kitchen, giving Teef and Jade some privacy. Before she could grab a cup from the cabinet, Jade has hung up and is off the phone.

"See, Jade. I told you that bastard wasn't going to admit to anything. He can't tell the truth to save his own damn life. Anyhow, are you about ready to get out of here and hit up this mall? I'm so excited. It has been ages since you and I went out and did girl shit together. I miss things like this so much."

"Taji, what are you talking about? You and Luna are always out somewhere shopping."

"Yes, I know, but that's me and Luna. Not you and me. Should I call my girls and have them meet us at the mall?"

"Yeah, you should. That would be fun. Then we can all come back here and get dressed and go to Ruth Chris."

"I know that we will all have a ball. My sisters get here the day after tomorrow, and we can do it all over again. I need to pamper myself more. All I do is work, work, work. I need this time because next week, the shenanigans will start. I'm already dreading it, but it must be done."

"He needs to know that I'm serious this time. I've forgiven him over and over but some shit you just can't come back from and being with a man is one of them. I mean, how in the fuck can I compete with that? I don't have a dick and I'm not about to go buy one either. That way, he's free to go spread his boochie cat as much as he wants."

Taji screams, "You caught that, huh?"

"I did, but I'd never heard that term before today."

"Yes, girl. That is what some men called their back entrance."

"Girl, I ain't never heard of such fuckery in my life, but that shit is funny as hell," Jade cackles.

"Anyway, I'm gonna go upstairs and call Luna and Kirsten and freshen up a little bit and then I'll be back down here and ready to go."

"OK, boo, I'm going to go back here and do the same."

They both take off in separate directions and in 15

minutes, they are done. Taji realized that whoever was in the home, gained entry through a window. This prompts her to go around to every window and door, checking to make sure that they are closed, secured, and locked. Once that is completed, they are out the door.

Once in the mall, Luna and Kirsten arrive and none of them hold back. They hit up store after store and they blow through a serious bag, with no regrets. They leave the parking lot feeling on top of the world because Lennox Square owes them nothing. After leaving the mall, they fight evening traffic while heading back to Taji's home. They return to the house and Taji notices that her bedroom light is on. She is not positive that she didn't leave the light on, so she tries not to ruin the night by over-thinking.

Once they enter, everything looks normal and there isn't anything out of place, so Taji begins to let her guard down and relax. Taji's house has six bedrooms and nine bathrooms, so each girl takes off in a different direction to go and get ready for tonight. They shit, shower, and bathe and one by one, each comes out looking like a bad bitch. It's like Taji is having her very own fashion show.

They make sure to show Jade extra love when she unveils her outfit. She looks gorgeous and so happy. This is how Taji always wants her friend to be. She deserves it. They head to Ruth Chris to enjoy a wonderful dinner and drinks. At dinner, Taji recommends going to the strip club afterwards to have a little naughty fun and all the girls agree. As long as it's not a bitches and switches type of club.

They all want to go somewhere classier, so they head to the Goldrush Showbar. While there, they are having the time of their lives. Jade lets her hair down. Taji pays a few of the dancers to take Jade to the champagne room and give her a private lap dance. Which she only agrees to after Taji promises to go with her. She does and after about six shots, Jade is completely at ease. She even feels on one of the dancer's booty and Taji screams with laughter. As the night comes to an end, all the girls hug, dance, and twerk, take pictures, then they all go their separate ways.

Jade and Taji are together of course, and Taji takes the liberty of saving both of their lives by driving home. She's horny as a toad and wants to slide off and get some beef-stick but doesn't dare leave her friend alone in her condition. Jade is blitzed, falling asleep within minutes of them pulling off from the club, and Taji knows then that her job as a friend for this day was done.

Once they arrive back home, Taji helps Jade out of her clothes and into bed just as Jade did for her in college. She's happy that she can be there to keep her friend safe and have her back. She undresses her and helps her get into her pajamas.

Once Jade is dressed and tucked in, Taji ascends the stairs to get herself situated. She starts with pinning her hair up and removing her make up then she hops in the shower. While bathing, she smiles and finds comfort in knowing that although her friend is about to face one of the biggest hurdles in her life, she's there to support her. Jade has always been there for Taji in a way that no other friend has. Often putting her needs aside for Taji's needs. No other incident reminds Taji of Jade's loyalty more than that terrible night in college. Jade dropped everything to be by her side.

Hindsight is twenty twenty and Taji wishes that she would have just listened to Jade from the beginning. Things might have turned out differently if she had. Finals were on that upcoming Monday and Jade and Taji were supposed to stay in studying the entire weekend. Taji grew bored and decided that she was going to go to a small house party for just a couple of hours. Then come back and hit the books for the rest of the night.

Taji left at 9:00 PM. and one of the girls that were supposed to go to the party with her backed out at the last minute. She decided to go alone, and that was one of the biggest mistakes of her life. While there, one of the guys drugged her and he and his friends took turns raping her well into the night. When 3:00 A.M. came and Taji wasn't back, Jade went to look for her and found her in the parking lot inside her car. She was in the passenger seat with her pants down with blood and semen all over her.

Taji was unconscious so she hopped in and drove her to the nearest hospital. They performed a rape kit. The doctors discovered severe vaginal tears and anal tears. Her stomach was pumped to keep her from getting alcohol poisoning. Charcoal was also administered to absorb some of the drugs that she had been given. Her toxicology report showed that she had the date rape drug in her system along with molly, ecstasy, methamphetamines, and Valium.

The people that did this to her gave her a cocktail that could have killed her, but luckily it didn't. Thank God for DNA analysis because two of the four guys were arrested. Those young boys went into that court room and started singing like canaries. The other two denied the allegations at first and since no DNA pointed at them, they let them go just to arrest them days later. They put their own nails in their coffins when a video of them raping Taji surfaced and they had no choice but to confess.

Taji was the talk of the town for a while. She almost dropped out of school because of *victim shaming*. It was by the Grace of God and Jade that she didn't. For the next couple of months after the incident, Jade practically did her work along with Taji's work so that she would not fail.

Taji had told Jade how much her mother sacrificed to send her to college and Jade didn't want her mother to have done it all for nothing. Her mother also encouraged her to come home but Jade promised Ms. Dawson that she would look after Taji. She was a woman of her word. She looked after her and much more. There were times that Taji was so depressed that she didn't want to get out of bed. Jade would practically drag her out, feed her, and make sure that she got to class on time. She remained solid for Taji, hence Taji's love and concern for Jade. Taji would protect Jade with her life if need be. That is her girl until the end of time.

CHAPTER 16

Protection

As Taji drifts off to sleep, her phone rings. She answers, but no one is on the line. She hangs up and it rings again. She can clearly hear someone breathing but not a word was spoken. She hangs up once again and blocks the number because she's not about to have anybody playing on her phone. She receives a text message from an unknown number.

> Unknown number: Why did you hang up on me? I know your Mama taught you better manners than that.

Pissed, she texts back.

> Me: I don't know who you are and what you want but I suggest that you find you somebody to play with. Don't call or text my damn phone anymore.

She sends the message and then blocks the number. Another text message comes through.

> Unknown number: I'm not playing at all. You should know that weak ass Ruger that you carry around is not scaring anybody.

She begins to feel sick on the stomach. Not many people know that she carries a gun and they definitely shouldn't know what kind. She gets up to turn on the light and her phone rings again.

She answers but doesn't say anything and neither do they. Just breathing. She hangs up and blocks that number as well. Within seconds, her phone rings again and she puts the phone on DND. Taji grabs her 45 from under her mattress and puts it in the bed with her. Starting to feel uneasy again, she gets up, puts on her house shoes, grabs her gun, and walks around the inside of the house to make sure that no one is there.

The house is over 6,000 square feet so it takes her some time. Taji doesn't have any fear. Just worry. She doesn't want to have to hurt someone but definitely will without a second thought. She thinks about heading to Jade's room to wake her but what good would that do? Jade acts like a frantic white woman at times plus she's pissy drunk so what would be the purpose?

Searching every square foot of the house she finds nothing. She returns to bed but doesn't turn off the lights. She is spooked and pissed. *Reggie needs a life*, she says to herself. She gets back in bed and falls asleep.

The next morning, Taji wakes up and checks her calendar. Today is the day that she promised Farod that she would stop by and visit. She knows that she has a lot going on but she dares not fuck that up. She wants to keep those bills on auto pay. After she's done seeing him, she plans on pulling up on Rico to see what's popping with him.

She still feels uneasy about the phone calls and texts from last night, but Taji has a way of pushing shit to the side and moving forward. She trots downstairs to check on Jade and she's not in her bed. She peeks outback and there she finds her and Bella out on the deck. Jade is smoking a cigarette and Taji is appalled.

"OOOOOh... bitch, I caught you. I thought you told me that you would never pick up another cigarette again and here you are. Joe Camel himself."

"Please don't judge me. I've been trying to keep it from you but girl, my nerves are shot. I just needed a few puffs."

"Jade, when did you start back smoking? I can't believe it. It's been years."

"I know, I know. I backpedaled. I bought a pack the day that I came over here. I've only had 2 since I bought them, but I woke up this morning because Reggie called me begging me to come home and he just plain worked my nerves. I just had to have something."

"That reminds me. Girl, last night while you were asleep, I started getting some weird phone calls and text messages. I can't say who they were from because they never said anything. All they did was sit on my phone, breathing all heavy and shit. Then when I blocked whoever it was, they started texting and calling from different numbers. That shit had me so spooked that I walked around this entire house with my gun waiting for a muthafucka to jump out. I was going to *rock a bye baby,* their asses."

"Girl, why didn't you wake me up?"

"For what, Jade? You wouldn't have been any help. Your ass is scared of your own shadow, the only thing that doesn't seem to scare you are those damn dead people."

"That's because my mama always told me that there was no reason to fear the dead. That I should fear the people walking around. The dead isn't going to do shit to me."

"I guess your mother is right, but still. Anyway, do you

have anything planned for today? I have got to do a little running around, but I'll be back later on tonight."

"That sounds like a little more than running around to me if you are going to be gone all day."

"That's the plan. I'm going to swing by and see Farod for a few and then the Puerto Rican Papi."

"Ohhh, Taji. I didn't know that you were still seeing Rico. I thought that you left him in 2024."

"Jade, you can fill a book up with shit that you don't know about me," Taji laughs. "Yes, my Papi is still around. We don't kick it as hard as we used to, but I do still see him from time to time."

"Ok, well, I guess I'll just lie around and try to recover from yesterday. I wanted to say thank you for orchestrating such a good time for me. I had a blast. I don't remember anything after the lap dance though. Did I embarrass myself?" she asks as she puts her cigarette out.

"Of course you didn't. Drunk or not, you always remain classy, Jade."

"That's good to know. The last thing that I want is my face on a photo shitfaced and acting a fool."

"We did take pictures, but we all agreed not to post any. They are strictly for our memories. Oh, you did feel on one of the dancer's ass though."

"Oh my God! Are you serious?"

"Yes, she had a big ole ass on her, too. It was nice and

soft. I could tell. If I were you, I'd probably would have grabbed a handful too," Taji giggles as they enter back into the house.

"Well, I'm going to head upstairs and get my day started. Do you want me to put on a cup of coffee before I go?"

"No, actually, I think that I will have some herbal tea."

"Ooooh fancy. I forgot that you'd rather have hot tea than coffee."

"Yes, and if I do have coffee, I like it iced. The only thing I need you to do is point me to your tea kettle."

"It's under the cabinet next to the stove."

"Thanks, boo."

"You're welcome. I'll come say goodbye before I leave."

Taji treks back upstairs and glances at the clock. It reads 12:33 P.M. Farod usually leaves the store for lunch around 2:00 so she gets a move on to catch him before he does. She wants to submerge her ass in the water but a shower will have to do.

She bathes thoroughly, gets out, and searches for something sexy to wear. She wants Farod to slob when his eyes land on her and she wants his brother to do the same. She chooses a slutty lace catsuit that she bought from Shein for roleplay with Lucas. Farod and his brother will get an eye full today.

The outfit leaves nothing to the imagination. The sides

are completely out and her ass will be as well. She slides on her outfit before doing her makeup and hair. She sprays on Farod's favorite perfume, Miss Dior, and heads downstairs to tell Jade goodbye.

Sipping her tea, Jade waves goodbye as she scrolls on her phone. Taji walks out the front door, heading to her car when her phone chirps. Another unknown number is texting her and she refuses to even look at it as she doesn't want her day ruined.

CHAPTER 17

It Aint Trickin'

Hopping in her car, she takes off, heading to the store. Pulling up, she sees Farod through the window. He takes one glance at her and smiles bigger than a kid in a candy store. Farod's store is in the heart of the hood so there are all kinds of unsavory characters around. Taji doesn't sweat it because she knows how to handle herself in any situation. She hops out of her BMW and the cat calls start in. She doesn't stop her strut. She's here for business and business only. A nice young man opens the door for her, she says thank you, and he slaps her on the ass.

Taji loses it, almost pulling out her Ruger, but she remembers where she is and decides against it.

"Young man, please don't ever put your muthafuckin'

hands on me again. I'm not the type of bitch to fuck with," she says, scowling through gritted teeth.

"My bad, ma'am... that ass is sitting nice, and I couldn't help myself," the young man mumbles.

"Well, you should try. Keep your hands to your damn self," she mutters as she makes eye contact with Farod.

"Hi there, honey pie, I was hoping to catch you before you went to lunch," she says as she wraps her arms around Farod's neck.

Farod's brother stares at Taji's ass and shakes his head in approval and that is all Farod wants. Her deed was done. She spends all of 10 minutes inside the store before she bids him ado and heads back to her car. The easiest money ever.

She races across town to Rico's place, calling him a few minutes before she arrives to tell him to open the door. He doesn't answer and this pisses her off, but she still goes, as she promised him that today is the day that she would visit.

Arriving in his driveway, she notices that there is another car present. She slides out her ride and knocks on the door. A beautiful woman answers.

"Ummm, hi, is Rico here?" Taji asks with a smile.

"Yes, he is. Who are you?"

"Well, if you must know, I am a friend of his. Are you going to get him or not?" Taji scoffs.

"Wait right here," she mutters as she slams the door in Taji's face.

I just know this bitch didn't. Who is this bitch?

Within a few seconds, Rico arrives at the door.

"Oh hey, I saw that you called and I was just about to call you back," he mumbles, as he comes out the door, closing it behind him.

"Oh, hey yourself. Who was that rude ass lady that answered the door?"

"She is a friend of mine, but I don't want you to be upset about it. I hadn't seen you in a while and I honestly didn't think that you were coming. I was calling you back to ask you to come another day if possible."

"Don't get me wrong, Rico. I'm not upset because you have someone here. I'm upset because you have someone here during the time that *I'm* supposed to be here. By all means, get yours. Just don't step on my toes to do so."

"I'm sorry, Taji. I should've called you before you drove all the way out here. I apologize for that. I will make it up to you. I promise. I will pay for your expenses as usual."

He pulls his phone from his pants pocket, presses a few buttons, and Taji's phone chimes.

"There you go. That should take care of any expenses that you incurred and a little something for yourself for the trouble."

"Thank you," Taji says as she turns and walks away, heading back to her car.

Once she gets back in, she takes a look at what he sent her and it was a $1000 payment. *Thank you very much, Rico,* she thinks to herself as she pulls off.

Her meet up with Rico was supposed to last all day long. Taji's left with nothing to do so she calls Jade.

"Hey girl, I'm on your side of town. I wanted to know if you want me to stop by your place and grab a few things for you. I know that Teef is at work. I can be in and out as long as you tell me where you need me to get things from."

"That would be awesome. I don't need much for now. Just some work clothes and you can find those hanging up in my closet. I also need more panties and bras. Oh, and can you go into the kitchen and grab that tin can with all of my expensive teas? It's in the cabinet with a picture of Big Ben on the front."

"Ok, is that all?"

"No. Can you look in my nightstand and grab my rose for me? Also, grab the silicone dildo right beside it."

"Are you sure that you want me to get that? What if your husband has been using it? The dildo I mean."

"Good point. It may be time for me to just go buy a new one," they both giggle. "That should be all though. Thank you so much, Boo. I'm still going over there next week, but that's all I need for now. Love you and I'll see you when you get back home. Wait. Before you hang up... I thought you were going to see Rico?"

"I did but things didn't go as planned and it's perfectly OK with me. He Apple Cash me $1000 for my time which was about three minutes so I'm good. I'm on my way back home after I pick up your things."

"Ok, see you soon," Jade says as she hangs up.

By the time Taji and Jade get off the phone, she's pulling up in Jade's driveway. Teef's car isn't in his usual parking space so she knows that he's away. She takes her keys out of her purse but still puts her purse on her shoulder because it has her Ruger inside. She doesn't want any surprises, but just in case she does run into issues, she has a way to protect herself.

She sticks her key into the lock and just as she's about to turn it, she stops and remembers that Jade has an alarm system.

"Dammit. I forgot to get the code from Jade."

She hears a voice behind her say, "Bitch, why do you need a code to my house?"

"First off... That is *the last* time you will ever call me *a bitch*. Secondly, your wife asked me to grab a few things for her. Now, if you're gonna have a problem with that, you're gonna have to take it up with her and you need to keep in mind that this is her house, too."

"You know, Taji, I never liked your ass. I could never

understand why she was friends with a slut like you. Even in college. All she talked about was Taji. You know I was glad when all of those boys fucked you and treated you like the slut that you are. I thought that you would get the fuck back to where you belong, the sticks, but instead, you stayed. You have made my life harder than it had to be by keeping my wife's head filled with bullshit about me."

"I never said one bad word about your punk ass until she did. You fucked up enough on your own. I didn't have to say shit. Now shut the fuck up talking to me. Let me get what I came here to get, so I can be on my way. If you value your life, you will keep your motherfucking hands and spit to yourself."

"Are you threatening me? Have you forgotten who I am?"

"That wasn't a threat at all. It is *a promise*, and I don't give a fuck about who you are or what you do."

Teef and Taji are standing face-to-face when the front door opens. The housekeeper stands there looking wide eyed, wondering what is going on.

Taji turns to her and utters, "Hello, Miss Alice. I'm sure you remember me. I am Jade's best friend. She sent me over here to get a few items for her. Would you mind grabbing her expensive teas from the cabinet while I get some of her things from her closet?"

"Ok sure, I don't mind at all," she says, as she opens the door wider and motions for Taji to come in.

Taji enters into the house and heads straight for the bedroom. She darts into the closet and comes out minutes later with seven outfits for her good sis. Teef is on her heels, supposedly making sure she doesn't take anything of his. She then turns her attention to the nightstand and retrieves the rose and lastly the bras and panties. As soon as she's done, she runs to the kitchen to grab the tin. Teef sneers at her as she walks right past him and out the door. Loading the things into the car, she notices that Teef is now back on the porch. As he watches her, she throws up her middle finger, hops in her ride, and burns rubber in his driveway. She pulls off and disappears from his sight.

CHAPTER 18

Dear Mama

Taji calls Jade as soon as she makes it up the street.

"Girl, that was a close one. I thought that I was going to have to put your husband on his back."

"What do you mean, are you ok?"

"Yes, boo. I'm fine. I'll tell you all about it when I get home. I just wanted you to be aware that I saw him while I was there and things got pretty heated so he's probably going to be calling you in a few minutes."

"You are right because that is him ringing in as we speak."

"Are you going to answer it?"

"No, I had enough of his shit this morning. I cursed him out and hung up the phone. He said something about how he knew that you had me over here dogging him out.

He also said that we would be back together if it weren't for you putting all kinds of negative shit in my head. He made me mad as hell because he acts like I can't think for myself. Hell, you didn't make him give me a VD. You didn't help me find his little box of nasties. All that shit was done by *him*, and he needs to learn how to take accountability. Everything is always someone else's fault. It's never Reggie's fault. He tries to treat me like he treats those criminals but that shit no longer works for me. I can already tell that this divorce is going to be horrible."

"Don't think like that. Everything is going to be fine. I'm going to stop and get us some wine and we will find something to binge watch. I'll be there in a little bit. See you soon," Taji says as she hangs up the phone.

Taji stops and grabs the wine and about 15 minutes later, she arrives home. Jade sees her pull up and meets her at the car to help her get her things. They enter back into the house and Taji makes a beeline to her room to get out of her catsuit and into something more comfortable. She descends back down the stairs and sashays into the kitchen to grab a wine opener and some glasses.

Jade is already in her night clothes. She never got out of them. They grab a few throws from the basket, some chips and popcorn, and take a seat on the couch. They decide on binging *The Last Days of Ptolemy Grey.* They get about three episodes in when Sapphire calls Jade to confirm pickup time for tomorrow. Jade and her sister talk for a while and just as she's about to hang up with her sister, Taji's phone rings. It's her mother's number, so she answers cheerfully.

"Heyyy, Mama, what are you doing?"

"Hello, Mama, are you there?"

"Mama, I can't hear you. Mama, are you there?"

Taji hangs up the phone and tries to call back but the line is busy. Her mama called her from the house phone so she calls her cell phone back. Her mother answers.

"Hey, baby, what's up?"

"Nothing much, Mama. I was returning your call. I was talking but I couldn't hear you."

"What do you mean returning my call? I didn't call you, baby. I'd been thinking about it but I hadn't gotten around to it."

"So, Mama, you didn't just call my cell phone from the house phone?"

"No, Shug, I didn't. I was in the kitchen cooking some vittles when I heard my cell phone ringing."

"Mama, somebody just called me from your house. Are you sure that it wasn't you?"

"Baby, I may be getting old but I'm not *that* old. Nor am I senile. I did not call you."

"Mama, I want you to get out of the house, **now!**" Taji yells in a panicked tone. "Somebody called me from your landline phone. I'm going to call the police. Don't hang up with me. Mama, just hold on for a second."

Taji grabs Jade's phone out of her hand and dials 911, giving them her mother's phone number and address, and asks if they could please send an officer over to search the house. She explains what happened and they agree to send someone. They take down Taji's number in case they need to call her back.

"Mama, are you still there?"

"Yes, I am. What is going on?"

"Mama, please get out of the house and go to the neighbor's house until the police gets there. Please, Mama. Don't fight me on this. I've been getting some strange threatening calls just like the one that came from your house. I can't risk something happening to you so please just go."

"Ok, ok, I'm turning off my stove and leaving."

"Good, thank you for listening, Mama. Let me know when you make it over there and you are safe."

In the background, Taji listens as her mom moves around and hears when what she assumes is the back door open and close, hearing wind blowing in the phone.

"Baby, I'm here. I'm standing on Mrs. Anderson's porch right now. She's letting me in. Can I hang up now?"

"No, Mama, not yet. Can you at least wait until the police arrive? Please."

"Ok, I will."

Taji proceeds to fill her mother in on what's been happening. She tells her that she thinks that its Jade's husband doing all of this, but she has no proof. By the time she explains everything, the police arrive. She begs her mother to call her back as soon as they conclude their search. She agrees and they disconnect the call. Taji is visibly shaken. Jade doesn't know what to do besides calling her husband to ask him if he's making these phone calls. Once again, he denies everything but neither Jade nor Taji believe him.

An hour later, Taji's mother, Jordan, calls back and advises Taji that everything was fine. The windows and doors were all locked up. The phone was working perfectly, and no one was in or around the premises. Taji breathes a sigh of relief, but the worrying doesn't stop there. Her mother convinces her that everything is ok and there's no need to fret.

"Taji, you must have forgotten. I have a 45, too, and I know how to use it, babygirl. Trust. You need not worry about your mama. I also have a 38 special in my room. A shotgun in the living room under the couch pillows and I carry a 9mm in my purse. You got this fancy alarm system, that I don't need, so I'll be fine. Nobody or nothing is going to see me before I see them. Child, I'm good. Now let me go so I can finish cooking my vittles. I'm starving."

"Ok, Mama, that makes me feel a little better. I love you and I will talk to you later."

"I love you too, baby. Goodnight."

Jade and Taji stare at each other, not knowing what to do or say. Neither of them feel comfortable about what just happened, but neither of them say so. They attempt to turn back on the television and watch as if nothing just happened, but their body language tells it all, causing Jade to break the silence.

"I know that you and Chosen are not on the best terms right now, but can't you call him and ask him to come over? I think both of us will feel safer if a man was here."

"You are right. We would, but I think Chosen has made it very clear that he doesn't want to hear from me. I'm not about to bother that man. Just like my mom, I have guns laying all around this place and I will use them. As a matter of fact, there is one in your room under your mattress. I suggest you get well acquainted with it."

"You mean to tell me that I've been sleeping on a gun all this time? I hate guns. When you do what I do for a living, you see the destruction that they cause. It's not pretty."

"I get that, Jade, I really do. But as a woman out here in these Atlanta streets, protecting yourself is necessary. My dad was a drug dealer, and there were always guns around growing up. I learned not to be scared of them. He took me out back at seven years old and let me fire one. You know living in the country, you can do that. Once he explained to me that it was needed to protect yourself, I was no longer afraid. He told me that there were some very bad people in the world that would hurt me just because of who I was and that I needed to know protecting myself was an option. Little did I know, *he* was one of those bad people, but that's another story for another day."

"Taji, my parents would never, but sometimes I wish they had."

"I tell you what. Tomorrow, after I get your sisters and we get acquainted, we will all go to the gun range so that you can learn how to shoot. I have enough guns in this house for everybody," Taji laughs.

"Did you forget that my sisters are felons? They can't be around guns like that."

"Damn, I sure did forget. I guess that is out of the question. You and I can go sometime when they leave. You aren't scared to go with me are you?"

"No, I'm not scared. I know you've got my back."

"I sure do, *like a chiropractic*," they both cackle.

"I'm feeling a little better so let's try to get through the rest of these episodes and then we can hit the hay. We've got a long day ahead of us tomorrow and it's already 10 PM," Taji announces.

They turn back on the television and continue watching episode after episode until they arrive at the end. They fist pound each other, fold up there throws, and head to bed.

Once Taji is in her room, she puts her phone on the charger, realizing that it is still on DND. Her mother was able to get through because she is on her favorites list. She takes the time to look through all of the messages and phone calls that she received. She can't believe her eyes. She has 47 missed calls and 92 text messages waiting on her. Each seemingly coming from a different number.

What in the fuck is really going on?

She is so disturbed by what she sees that she doesn't open any of the messages. Taji despises the police but is seriously thinking of calling them because this is getting out of hand. She pushes that thought to the side and starts thinking of some dick. Getting her rocks off with Rico would have taken the edge off, but since that wasn't possible, she remains tense as ever. She could really use some thug loving so she calls Motion to see where he is and what he's doing.

"What's up, stranger?" Motion quips as he answers the phone.

"Missing you is all. Are you busy?"

"A little bit. Sitting here talking to my homies about some shit we've got going on. What's up with you? It's been a minute since you've hit me up. I thought you forgot all about me."

"Now Motion, how could I *ever* forget about you? Seriously though, it's not like that. I've just had a lot going on these past couple of weeks. I would love to see you though."

"Say less. I'm on the way."

Taji jumps up and hops in the shower. She washes her kitty down to the ground. Once she is done bathing, she dries off and heads straight to her lingerie drawer. First, she grabs two condoms and puts them on her nightstand. Then she finds a black lace negligee with the crotch cut out, a garter belt, and black pumps. She moisturizes, then sprays her body down with Baccarat Rouge. Sliding the negligee on she patiently wait to see those lights hit the driveway.

CHAPTER 19

Slow Motion

The lights from the driveway illuminate her room and she runs downstairs to meet him at the door. He is looking great but smells like a pound of loud. She hates that smell. She grabs his hand and leads him through the darkness up to her room. Walking into the bedroom, he attempts to kiss her neck, and she declines.

"Motion, you know I really want to do this, but I can't with the weed smell. If you want me like I want you, you would go in there and take a shower and brush your teeth. Look under the sink, there are brand new toothbrushes under there. I need you fresh like me, bae."

"Girl, you ain't said shit but a word. I've been out and about all damn day. I'd be happy to get in that fancy ass shower. Shiddd, girl. Hand me a rag and a towel and give me about 20 minutes and I'm all yours."

She does as she's told and hands him a rag and towel. Motion treks his way into the bathroom. Taji lies across the bed, waiting for him to finish. While she waits, she notices her phone is lighting up. She rolls over to get a glimpse. Another text message has just come in. Since she's not alone, she picks up the phone to read it.

> Unknown number: So, you fuck with street trash now? I would have never taken you for that type. Especially not living the way that you live. Are you not scared that he will rob you?

She throws the phone down, scared shitless because now she knows that she is being watched. She instantly feels nauseous.

"I don't know who this is, but I wish that this mutha-fucka would leave me alone already."

"Who are you talking about, baby?" Motion asks as he steps back into the bedroom.

"I don't know who I'm talking about and that's the damn problem," she says as she picks her phone up from the bed and let's Motion see the text messages.

"What the fuck? Rob you? Who is this clown ass nigga?"

She sits Motion down and explains what has happened in the last week. Motion is furious because he knows that Taji doesn't bother anybody. He knows that her priority is minding her business and getting money, not inserting herself into bullshit. He asks what Jade's husband's name is and she tells him. She also tells him that he's the D.A. That doesn't move Motion because titles don't scare him. He has a title of his own. He can tell that she's fucked up behind all this because her eyes don't have that same glimmer that he's used to. He hands her a pill and tells her to calm down. She refuses to take it because she doesn't do drugs at all. He offers her weed, which she doesn't mind, but she hates the smell. He digs in his pocket and comes out with a brand new vape pen.

"I was going to give this to my mama, but you need it more than she does. She doesn't like the weed smell either, but she loves being high," he chuckles.

"Thank you, Motion, now this I can do."

Taji takes a deep drag and coughs until her lungs hurt.

"Hold on, baby. That's not a regular joint so you can't puff it like one. You've got to suck it straight into your lungs and let it out. That way you won't cough like that."

She tries again and this time it's much smoother. She takes two more puffs and her shoulders begin to drop. All the tension melts away like an ice cube in Florida at high noon. She feels lighter than she has in a week. As the tension melts, the lust rises.

She lights a candle and turns the light off. Motion lies back on the bed and all she sees is the silhouette of his huge dick and it turns her the fuck on. Climbing on the bed, she mounts him like a stallion. Motion kisses and licks her neck, grabs her by her waist, and pushes her down while she grinds her clit against his swollen dick. He tries to slide it into her snatch, but she doesn't let him. She wants to tease him and drive him nuts as only she could do.

By now, Motion usually would have taken charge, but he lets her do her thing, considering what she's been through. He raises up and finds her lips. With his tongue, he traces her mouth before their tongues unite. Taji feels his dick growing harder and harder beneath her. Motion slides his arms around her back and then flips her over.

Diving face first into her pussy, he gets 10's across the board. His tongue feels magnificent, pure delectation. Because of the weed, everything is enhanced. Every touch, smell, sound is magnified by three and he takes full advantage. He licks and sucks her swollen clit and forces her to cum in his mouth. She yelps from the pleasure and Motion can't take it anymore. His tongue has tasted her enough. It's time for his dick to get some action.

She slides down and takes him into her mouth as she cuffs his balls. They begin to tighten with each slurp of the tongue. She knows what's next and she doesn't want him to cum prematurely, so she stops. Reaching over to grab a condom, she rips it open and slides it onto his dick in one swipe. She climbs back on top of him and grinds on him until he is about to lose it. She slides left, then right, and lines her slit up perfectly to receive his manhood. He moans so loud and high pitched that she is startled.

"Fuck, Taji. Slow down please."

"Awwww Motion, what do you mean slow down? I've only bounced on your dick twice. I can't go any slower than that."

"Well whatever you are doing, just stop because I can't take that shit. Girl, you've got that serious water."

"Dont...Tell...Me...That...You....Are...About...To...Cum?" she says with each bounce on his dick.

Motion recoils so hard that he almost throws her off him. He sighs and groans and tries to pump with the gummy-worm. Defeated is the best way to describe it. They both lie in bed laughing.

"Motion, please don't hit me with the gummy-worm. Just stop humping, baby. All the fire power is gone," Taji laughs.

"I know, Taji, but I hate to go out without a fight."

"Boo, you lost. Just take your L. It's ok. There's always next time."

"Hell, you know what it is. Next time ain't gonna be no different. Girl, that water gets me everytime. I can't handle it and I swear I be doing everything possible to stay in it. I fail like hell, don't I?"

"Yes, you do but you are still ok with me. You get me right before you give out of fire power so I could never be mad." They both giggle.

"Yeah, but you call me because you wanted that thug loving. That ain't what that was at all."

Taji cackles as she lies down on his chest, becoming silent.

"Bae, are you going to sleep?"

"No, Motion, just thinking about Teef and all the shit the has been going on. I'm tired and my bestie is tired, too. That nigga has done her wrong for so many years. Now he's got the nerve to be fucking with us because she doesn't want his ass anymore. I swear, that girl did everything that she could to stay in that marriage. She ignored every red flag that there was. Each time she did, he got worse and worse and became so disrespectful. My girl doesn't deserve any of this shit and neither do I."

"Taji, I don't want you to worry about him. I got him. Just sit back and chill."

"That is easier said than done when you know that a nigga is watching you. I don't feel good about that at all. I've had enough creep shit happen to me in my life. I'm not about to let it happen again and that's on my soul."

"You can relax, I promise. Nobody is going to fuck

with you or her. You can bet that. Consider your problems handled. Now let me get my ass on up and get out of here. I told the homies that I would be back in a little bit so it's time for me to roll," he says as he gets up and slides on his underwear.

"I knew that you weren't going to stay that long. You've got shit to do. They don't call you Motion for nothing."

CHAPTER 20

No Bougie Shit

Motion leaves and Taji is still high as a kite. Sleep finds her without even trying. The next morning, Jade wakes up before Taji and goes upstairs to find her. Taji is knocked out and spread diagonally across the bed. She has no cover on, her pussy is hanging out the side of her lingerie as well as her titties. Jade laughs and shakes her head.

"Tajiiiiii... Taji, wake up girl. It's almost time for you to go and get my sisters."

"Huhhhh," Taji groans.

"Wake up, girl. You've got to go and get Sapphire and Diamond. It's almost 7:00 A.M. and their flight lands at 8:30. You know how this Atlanta traffic is and even worse, how busy the damn airport is. You need to get up or you are going to be late getting them."

"Ok, I'm about to get up now. Just give me five more minutes," Taji begs as she rolls over and tucks the pillow under her neck.

"No, Taji, no. Get up, and why are you dressed like a damn cabaret dancer? Did you have company come over last night after I went to sleep?"

"Jaaaaade, why are you so nosy?" Taji laughs as she sits up in the bed. "Yes, I had company last night. I needed something that would take the edge off and that *something* did."

"Ohhhh shit. Gimme all the details," Jade mutters as she walks into the room and takes a seat on the chaise.

"I don't have time, remember? I've got to go and get your sisters."

"Girl, stop. You can talk and get ready at the same time. Now spill the beans."

"Ok. After I came up here to go to bed, I couldn't get what's been going on out of my head. I looked at my phone and realize that I had a ridiculous amount of missed calls and text messages. That had me on edge, then once my company came over, another text message came through. This one fucked me up because it proved that we are indeed being watched."

"Why do you say that?"

"Because whoever it was, saw the nigga get out of his car."

"Oh my goodness, Taji, are you serious?" Jade mutters as she covers her mouth.

"Hell yes, I'm serious. I wouldn't make no shit like that up."

"So what are we going to do about it?"

"Don't you worry about anything. It is being handled. Anyway, I need to hop in and out the shower so I can get a move on. I hate going to this damn airport. Hopefully, they will come right out and I won't have to wait very long."

"Should I just stay here until you all get back? Or should I come after you arrive to make it look like I came over?"

"I think that it will be OK if you are just here when we get here. You have a key to my house so there's no need to act like you just arrived."

"Ok. I'm gonna go in here and clean my room so it doesn't look as messy. I want things to go perfect this weekend but above all, I want us to have a great time. Thank you again for doing all of this. I feel like you are going out of your way for me and I appreciate you so much."

"Jade, please stop thanking me. I haven't done anything that you wouldn't do for me. Girl, if it wasn't for you, I probably wouldn't be alive today and that's real talk. While your ass is standing there, why don't you make yourself useful and find me something comfortable to put on while I go get in the shower?"

"Ok, I'll find something and lay it on your bed. If you need me, I'll be in my room cleaning up."

"Thank you," Taji yells from the bathroom.

Jade finds Taji a comfortable two-piece, Juicy Couture set and a pair of Brooks that she has stuffed away in her closet. Then she goes downstairs to straighten out her room. Once Jade hits the bottom step, she hears a noise. She calls Bella's name and she comes running straight into Jade's arms. She hears the noise again. It sounded like a loud bump. She doesn't move an inch, waiting to see if she hears it again. She doesn't so she continues to her room.

Once Taji is dressed, she books it out the front door, screaming, "Bye Jade," as she runs to her car. She's short on time and she knows it so she fights traffic to make it to the airport on time. She does and they walk out about three minutes after she pulls up.

She pops her trunk so that they load their luggage. Taji looks on through the rearview mirror because she doesn't do manual labor. They get in and the shenanigans start. These girls are just as loud and boisterous as Taji remembered.

"So, sis. Tell me the real deal about this Reggie nigga. Are we gonna have to fuck him up? He hasn't put his hands on my sister, has he?" Sapphire asks.

"No, he hasn't put his hands on her, but he spit on me. I was out for blood, but it's being handled so none of us have to worry about him for the weekend. We can actually enjoy ourselves, and you two can give your sister the love that she needs and spend quality time with her. I told you on the phone that we were going to have a girls' weekend, and we are. I've got a chef coming, a nail tech, and a masseuse."

"See Taji, you are with that bougie shit. We are in Atlanta girl. We don't want to stay in the house all day long. Go ahead and cancel that shit and we will do like regular people do. Go out to eat, go get our nails and feet done, and go get a massage. We don't need anybody to come to us. We outsiiiiiide," Diamond and Sapphire scream.

"OK, if that is what you want, I will go ahead and cancel it. Y'all bitches are making me lose money because it's too late for me to get my deposit back, but I understand what y'all are saying. Oh, I was able to get her to go out to a strip club with me and a few other girls the other night. She had a ball but don't tell her that I told you. She would be so embarrassed. I got her fucked up and paid for her to get a lap dance. She doesn't remember most of it, but she let her hair down for the first time in a long time."

"See Taji, I love that a bitch like you has my sister's

back," Diamond says. "We are going to get litty this weekend and I can't wait."

CHAPTER 21

We Outside

Taji drives until she spots Hardees. Pulling into the drive-through, she orders breakfast sandwiches, hashbrowns, and drinks for everyone. They make it back to the house and once again Jade is on the porch. Seeing the BMW pull up, Jade immediately takes off running and screaming towards her sisters. It looks like a scene off the *Color Purple*. They hug each other dearly, grab everything from the trunk, and run into the house. Taji looks around at her surroundings and can't help but wonder if she's being watched.

Once inside, Taji shows them to their rooms and gives them a full tour of the house. She hardly ever goes to the other side of her home. Unless she's showing the cleaning lady something that she would like to have done. So, she just about forgets what some of the rooms look like. Once they are done touring the home, they enter back into the kitchen to eat the breakfast that Taji purchased. She makes mimosas to go along with breakfast and they begin to plan their day. Jade is giddy as a school child and is really happy to see her sisters.

Jade attempts to tread lightly when it comes to conversations surrounding her husband and home. When her sister, Sapphire, asks how Reggie was, her reply is simply, "Good." Taji looks over at Jade and can see the nervousness on her face. She mouths "relax" and Jade tries to fix her face. Her sisters ask her another question and Jade gives in and explodes. Her truth becomes the shrapnel.

"Ummm, y'all. I didn't want to tell you two this way but I'm just gonna come out and say it because I'm no good at keeping secrets. Plus, it's not my shame to bear. Reggie and I are getting a divorce," Jade blurts out. "That son of a bitch gave me a disease and I am sick and tired of his ass. I'm leaving him. I'm staying with Taji for now, but I just want to let you know that I'm ok. I'm keeping my head up and I know that I'm going to be fine. Before you ask, no, I don't need either one of you to beat anybody's ass. He's probably getting his ass spanked as we speak."

"Hold up," Diamond quips. "What the hell does that mean?"

"It means that I think that he is cheating with a man. I

found some freaky shit in the attic. There is no explanation for it other than he's gay."

"Well damn, Taji, you didn't tell us that."

Taji looks at Diamond and shakes her head *no*.

"Oops..." Diamond says. "I'm sorry, I didn't mean to say that. Please don't be mad at Taji, she just wanted to help."

"Please don't be upset with me, Jade. I told them because I knew you wouldn't. You need them, not to beat Teef's ass or anything, but to help love you through it. To be honest, if I had Onyx's number, I would've called him and told him, too."

Taji braces herself for Jade's meltdown but Jade just sits silent.

"So you mean to tell me that *you* called them and asked them to come? Let me guess, *you* paid for the tickets and everything, didn't you?"

"Yes," Taji says as she takes a sip of her mimosa and sinks down into her chair.

Jade burst out laughing. "I should have known because there was no way that these cheap bitches would ever fly Delta. Spirit is their go to," Jade cackles as she slaps the table, tickled as ever.

They all burst out laughing.

"So, you aren't mad at me?"

"Girl, no. You did all of this for me because you want

to see me happy. How could I ever be mad at you for having my mental health in mind? You love me and you are always looking out for me. It's hard to be mad at you, Taji," she says as she leans over and hugs her.

"Whew! I'm glad to hear that because I thought that I overstepped."

"You did but you meant well and that is what matters. Your intentions were good," Jade mutters.

"Oh, and Taji, you don't have to worry about calling Onyx. We've already done that, so he knows. Now, everything is out in the open. Now that we've had that Kumbaya moment, can we get this party started? We are ready to get out in these ATL streets," Sapphire quips as she rubs her hands together.

"I thought that we were going to stay in. Taji has some nice things planned for us," Jade expresses.

"Not anymore, these whores made me cancel. Girl, you know that these two don't like to sit in one place for too long. You heard them, they want to be in the streets."

"Well to the streets we go, I guess." Jade verbalizes in a dry tone.

Once they are done with breakfast, everyone speeds off to get ready. Taji decides that she isn't going to change. She will save her good clothes for later. Besides, she looks cute in her little Juicy outfit anyway. Jade is fully dressed as well, so she sits in the living room waiting for her sisters to come back down. Although she is in one of the worse phases of her life, she still feels blessed.

She thinks back on her life, her sisters' lives, and becomes overwhelmed with happiness because she's glad that they made it out of the system. They are now making something of themselves. Jade is the youngest of the four but feels like a proud mother when she looks at them. Mixed with happiness, there is also a tinge of sadness. A chapter of her life is coming to an end. She loved a man with every fiber of her being, but it never seemed good enough. Jade wanted unconditional love, romance, and duality with the person that she thought that she would spend the rest of her life with. But as she told Taji earlier, God laughs when we make plans. She can't even begin to think of what is next in her life. Jade knows that she's going to have to take things day by day. She has already begun grieving her marriage before it ends.

Her sisters saunter downstairs looking like two country bumpkins. Jade looks, smiles, and tells them that they look nice. She then calls for Taji. Taji comes down the stairs and they are ready to pounce. They all hop into Jade's Infiniti SUV because it's roomier and take off.

One by one they knock off everything planned. They start with shopping at the mall and flea markets, then the nail salon, then the masseuse, and end the night at The Cheesecake Factory. Jade's sisters always wanted to go because they've never been but heard great things.

Taji was cool with that because she really wasn't dressed for anything else. She hated the thought of heading back home to change clothes and coming back out and so did the other girls. They enjoy a nice dinner full of laughs, reminiscing, and reflecting. A time was had, but they are exhausted and ready to head back home.

Jade whips into Taji's driveway and Taji observes a car in the empty lot next to her house. The others don't seem to notice but she does of course. She's the one on edge these days.

"Hey, do any of you all see anybody in that car over there?"

"We can't see shit, Taji. The windows are dark as hell. Do you want me or Sapphire to go over there and check it out?"

"No, Diamond you will not," Jade gripes. "You are not about to get into any shit while you are here. It's only day one."

"Girl. hush, hell, I'm the big sister. I don't need your little ass telling me what to do. Now if Taji needs me to go and check it out, I will."

"No, Diamond, your sister is right. It's not a big deal.

I've just never seen that car before. That's all. It's all good. Let's go on in the house and get this party started." Taji exclaims while trying to play it cool. She's worried but doesn't show it.

CHAPTER 22

Stay Ready

H opping out of the car in a great mood they strut into the house. They run to their rooms to freshen up and slide on their matching pajamas that Taji purchased for them. Then they meet back in the living room. Sapphire immediately connects her phone to the Bluetooth speaker to set the mood. *Let Her Cook* by Glorilla, blares through the speakers and everyone does a jig. Taji enters the kitchen to start making drinks and Jade follows right behind her. They both play bartender, asking Sapphire and Diamond for their drink of choice. They both yell, "Hennessy," in unison and Jade and Taji look at each other and laugh.

"Girl, your sisters act like straight up niggas. I thought they were going to say something like Apple Crown or an amaretto sour. Something less harsh but these heifers want hair on their damn chests," Taji chuckles.

"They've always been like that. They like that hard shit. They used to get in trouble when we were little for going in our uncle's stash. We didn't have alcohol in our house growing up, but my auntie and uncle did. Every time we went over there, they would hit up their liquor cabinet. If you had some corn liquor, they would probably drink that shit, too," Jade giggles. "I always thought that my sisters were too pretty to be as hard as they are. I mean Taji, can you imagine being a man and approaching one of them? Their outside definitely doesn't match their inside."

"Well, Jade, both did do hard time so maybe that's why they play no games. I know one thing. They are not with the shits. I wouldn't dare fight either one of their asses. They are the type of bitches that you have to shoot." Taji chuckles as she grabs two glasses, pouring Henny on the rocks.

They finish making their drinks and join Sapphire and Diamond in the living room. Jade tells Sapphire to quiet the music for a minute so that she can make a toast.

"I want to take the time to thank God for this reunion and the support and love of family. I am so happy that you two decided to hop on that plane and come to see your little sister. I need you guys more than you will ever know and I am so thankful for y'all. Y'all work my nerves sometimes, but I wouldn't trade neither one of you crazy girls for the world."

"We wouldn't trade you either," Diamond says. "You are our little sister, and we always got your back. We ain't scared of naan nigga walking this earth and we would literally die for you. NOW TURN MY SHIT BACK UUUUPPPPP," she yells as she grabs the arm of the sofa and starts hunching it. They all burst out laughing.

The four of them knock back drink after drink while dancing, singing to the top of their lungs, rapping, and twerking. They turn Taji's house into their own dance club. Having a ball until Jade passes out drunk. Which is no surprise considering she's the lightweight of the group. Sapphire helps Jade to her bedroom and lies her across the bed, then decides that she, too, is tired and is taking it in for the night.

They all bow out one by one with Taji being the last one standing. As the house grows quiet, Taji drags herself into the kitchen to clean up and wash the dishes. She thinks of Chosen because if he were there, she wouldn't have to do any of this. Since he isn't, she shrugs her shoulders and gets started. The fact that she must make her decision tomorrow still doesn't sit right with her. She attempts to think of ways to keep him around while not totally committing herself to him. She comes up empty handed. Taji knows that right now, she doesn't want to belong to just one man. Being around Jade and seeing what she's dealing with helps her solidify that decision. She decides that she will not be pressured into doing anything that she doesn't want.

Goodbye Chosen, she whispers to herself, as she wipes the countertops down. She turns the kitchen light off and treks to her bedroom. As Taji puts her dirty clothes away and straightens up her bedroom, she notices pieces of broken glass on her bathroom floor. She walks over to inspect further and realizes that it is one of her perfume bottles. She doesn't remember using the fragrance, in fact, it's one that she doesn't care for and was tucked behind her favorites. This observation sends chills down her spine because if she hadn't bothered it, then who did? Her mind goes to Jade. She wonders if she used it while she went to the airport to get her sisters. It's totally possible. Taji retrieved Jade's essentials from Jade's home but no smell good. So, maybe, just maybe Jade came upstairs to borrow it. She doesn't want to wait til' morning for an answer, so she runs down the stairs straight to Jade's room.

Taji shakes her vigorously. "Jade, wake up for a second. I need to ask you a question."

"Whaaaaat, Taji? I'm drunk girl. I don't feel like talking."

"This is serious, Jade... I just need to ask you one question and then you can go back to sleep. Did you use my perfume this morning while I was gone? The one in the clear glass bottle shaped like a rose?"

"No, Taji, I haven't been in your room. Now leave me alone!" she mumbles as she rolls back over, attempting to find a comfortable spot again.

"Ok, I'm sorry to have bothered you. I just needed to know. Go back to sleep, boo."

Jade runs into the kitchen to get a broom and dustpan and nervously heads back upstairs. As she enters the bedroom, her phone rings. Sick and tired of being scared in her own home, she answers and yells, "Fuck nigga. I don't know who and where you are but if I catch you in my house, I'm gonna blow your muthafuckin' head off. Whoever got you fucking with me must didn't tell you what kind of woman I am. I'm not the one to fuck with."

"Is that so?" a deep mysterious voice responds.

"Yes, it is so. Now who the fuck is this?"

"You will find out soon enough. You and all of your hoodrat ass friends will find out," the voice says and hangs up.

The phone call puts her in a state of panic but makes her more diligent than ever. She now knows that her every move is being watched but she has no way to prove it. She thinks of ways to get rid of this son of a bitch as she sweeps the glass from the floor. She's more pissed than anything because in this moment she feels helpless. Without wanting to get the police involved, her options are few. Motion told her that the problem was being handled.

She knows that things like this take time, but she needs this shit to be over like yesterday. Taji is all about keeping a low profile and keeping the peace. This situation doesn't allow her to not give a damn because not giving a damn and throwing caution to the wind could cost her more than she's willing to pay. Today has been a long day, she's tired, and she wants to sleep but can't.

Instead, she locates all her guns and cleans them. She also finds all the ammunition, loading each gun and their magazines. She gets her prize possession, an AK47 from under her bed and leans it against her nightstand. This was a gift from Motion. Actually, the gift that she loves most.

Taji feels ready for everything. By the time she finishes cleaning and oiling all guns, it's 5:00 A.M. She pulls the comforter back, grabs her 45, tucks it under the pillow, and goes to lala land.

CHAPTER 23

Can You Help Me

Taji wakes up to the smell of bacon and pancakes. She grabs her robe and heads to the kitchen. Sapphire, Jade, and Diamond are all there listening to Anita Baker and grooving on this lazy Sunday.

"Hey, sleepyhead, we thought that we would have to come drag you out of bed," Jade cheerfully says.

"What time is it?" Taji asks.

"It's almost noon. We've all been up for about an hour, but I just knew that once you smelled the food in the air that you would run your ass down here. It took you long enough. You have messed around and let the food get cold," Jade mutters.

"I was up busy after y'all went to bed, Jade. I was

cleaning and loading all my guns. Some freaky shit is going on around this house and I'm not with it. I think that somebody has been coming here while we are gone. Hell, while we are here for all I know."

"Why do you say that?" Jade asks.

"Because I found a broken perfume bottle in my bathroom last night. A perfume bottle that I never use. Do you remember me coming into your room last night to ask you about the bottle?"

"No, I can't say that I do. Girl, I was drunk drunk. I don't remember nothing," Jade confesses.

"I came in your room and asked you if you'd been in my bathroom and if you used the perfume. You told me that you hadn't been up there."

"This is true because I haven't."

"Well, that means somebody else *has*. There was a shattered bottle on the bathroom floor. Someone had to throw it to the floor because those perfume bottles are thick and they don't break that easily. There were big chunks of glass everywhere. Then the fucker called my phone and when I asked who the fuck it was, he said that we would find out soon enough."

"Wait... wait... wait..." Sapphire interrupts. "Who the fuck is *we* because we just got here?"

"I'm telling you. Whoever it is, is watching my house.

He knew when my company pulled up the other night. He could see how he looked and everything. He said me and my hoodrat ass friends would find out who he was soon enough so he knows that I'm not in this house alone. This shit is getting annoying and I'm ready to take it to another level if I have to. Nobody, and I do mean nobody, is going to ruin my peace or run me out of my own damn house."

"Do you think that your brother could help me in any kind of way? I mean he's FBI, right? He for sure can do something or at least point me in the right direction," Taji eagerly asks.

"Why don't you ask him yourself? He should be here in about an hour, and I know after hearing about these threats, he's going to be heated," Diamond states.

"Wait, are y'all playing with me? Is my brother really coming?" Jade queries in an excited tone. "Why didn't you two heifers tell me?" Jade screams as she hugs her sisters.

"Because it was supposed to be a surprise but since Taji needs help, I want her to know that she doesn't have to wait long to get it. Seems like it's a great thing that he's coming. Not only for you, Jade, but for Taji, too. Taji, this is indeed some weird shit. Do you still think that it is Reggie?"

"At first, I did but now, I'm not so sure. I would hate to think that his big teeth ass would take things this far, but I still don't trust him. The nigga did spit in my face and any man that can do that, has to hate me. I know one thing though, when it comes to my safety, I don't fuck around. We are going to get to the bottom of this one way or another. Since we are having a guest, I'm going to take a few pieces of this bacon and this dry ass pancake and go back upstairs. I need to be presentable." Taji says as she bites her bacon while sashaying up the stairs.

Taji wastes no time getting in the shower. She shaves her legs, throws a mask on her face, and scrubs her body for old and new. She doesn't remember too much about Jade's brother. She only saw him once and it was from a distance. She wants to impress him in the best way possi- ble. She becomes excited at the thought that all this bull- shit may be coming to an end.

Hopping out of the shower, she walks into her closet to put together a comfortable ensemble. She gets dressed and slaps her hair into a messy bun, making sure to leave her wavy baby hairs out. She wants to give sexy but not eager sexy. Effortless sexy and she pulls it off beautifully. She squirts a few sprays of her *Versace Dylan Blue* perfume and just as she finishes up, her doorbell rings.

Her first reaction is to run downstairs and tell all her business to Onyx in a desperate plea for help. After second thought, she realizes that Jade and her sisters haven't seen their brother in years. She doesn't want to interrupt their bonding time and make it all about her. She decides to wait awhile before heading back downstairs. While she waits, a text message comes through.

> Unknown number: Damn bitch. You really are a slut. You always have a nigga showing up at your crib. At least this one looks like he may have something to offer. But he's alone. Are all four of y'all going to take turns fucking him?

She hates to interrupt their family reunion, but Taji runs downstairs with the phone in her hand and runs straight to Onyx.

"Onyx, I'm in trouble, I'm being stalked and watched, and I could really use your help. Look at my messages and my call history. Please tell me that you can help me. Oh, and it's nice to meet you. I'm Taji, Jade's best friend, and welcome to my home."

Jade, Sapphire, and Diamond awkwardly stare at Taji because this is their first time seeing her rattled by anything.

They all chime in to tell Onyx what has been happening lately and he listens to every word. Taji was so wrapped up in seeking help that she failed to notice how fine Jade's brother is. He's a little bit older but that's a plus in her eyes. More stable and less games. Onyx is about 6'3", a solid 230 pounds. He's dark chocolate and super clean cut. The name Onyx fits him perfectly. He looks as if the sun comes down every day at high noon and French kisses him until dusk. Taji has never referred to any man as beautiful, but that is the only way to describe Onyx. He has beautiful white teeth with big hands and feet. Big brown bedroom eyes. Eyes that seem to peer through your soul and see all your past lives with one glance. After Taji takes in all his beauty, she relaxes and takes a seat on the sofa right next to him.

"See, do you see what I mean? He has to be watching me, watching us," she mutters as she points around the room at his sisters. "I've had enough of this shit. He calls and texts all day long. I have to put my phone on DND just to get some peace. Please tell me that you can help me."

"Before I do anything, I want to say thank you for inviting me to your beautiful home. It really is lovely. Of course I will try to help you. Especially if my sisters are involved. Let me make a few phone calls and see what I can do. Do you mind if I hold onto your phone for a minute?"

"No, I don't mind at all. Keep it as long as you need to. Maybe he will call or text while you are here, and you can see this creep in action. Before you make your phone call, let me show you to your room."

Taji grabs Onyx's hand and leads him up the stairs as Jade and her sisters shake their heads. Taji knows what Jade is thinking and she's right but she really isn't on that right now. Taji's main focus is finding out who's harassing her. As Taji and Onyx reach the top of the stairs, she releases his hands and motions for him to step into the bedroom where he will be staying. He walks in, drops his bags, and closes the door.

CHAPTER 24

Here For Good

"Taji, I need to speak with you privately for a moment if you don't mind. Will you please have a seat?"

She obliges and is shocked at herself for following his instructions with no lip.

"Ok, now my sisters are known for leaving out pertinent details but I need for you not to make that mistake. Do you know of anyone that may want to hurt you? Have you been beefing with anyone, male or female lately? I need you to think hard about this because it's super important. Usually when something like this happens, it's almost always someone that you know."

"No, Onyx. I haven't been into it with anyone besides Teef."

"Who is Teef?"

"Oh, I'm sorry. You know him as Reggie."

Onyx cracks up laughing. "So do you call the brother Teef to his face?"

"Not normally but when he pisses me off, then hell yes."

"And are you sure that he's the only one? Have you had any breakups lately? Friendship or relationships? Anyone you left or left you and may be pissed because of it?"

"Onyx, I don't get left. I do the leaving, except for Chosen," she says while looking away. "My long time guy *friend* gave me an ultimatum. He wants me to someday be his wife and I'm not ready for that just yet so I plan on saying goodbye to him but Chosen isn't crazy. He wouldn't do no shit like this."

"How can you be so sure and why don't you want that? Are you scared of commitment or something?"

"Onyx, I'm sure because I know him like the back of my hand. As far as your other question, can you tell me what that has to do with anything?"

"Nothing actually. I just want to know for myself."

"Well since you're asking, I'm not afraid. I'm just not going to be pressured to do anything that I don't want to do. I'm not ready to be married and tied down and I haven't met anyone that makes me want to change my mind."

"I see," Onyx retorts as he looks down at the floor. "Ok, well back to the subject. Can you tell me more about Reggie? I know that he isn't doing right by my sister but besides cheating, is he into anything else?"

"Onyx, he's the D.A. There is no telling what he's got going on. I want you to name one person who's fond of the D.A. Nobody likes their asses."

"I guess you've got a point there," Onyx murmurs. "Well, I've got to do my own intel. I need to make a few phone calls to try to get all this sorted out, but I'll be back down when I'm done. Tell my sisters to hold tight."

"Will do and thank you again. I know that you didn't come here for this, but I sure do appreciate it. Hopefully, we can get this thing sorted and over with and then you can have some time with your sisters. You only have one more day with Sapphire and Diamond because they leave soon. How long will you be staying?"

"I'm here for good. My headquarters were originally on the west coast but I've changed positions. I've taken a job right here in the city. I was so happy when my sisters called and asked me to come. I'd planned on coming here anyway so that I could find a place but my sisters aren't aware. I'm going to surprise them with that information very soon. Please don't tell them."

"I would never ruin your surprise like that. Your sisters

miss you terribly. They are going to be so excited to know they you are this close." *And so will I.*

"I know they are. This way, I can keep a better eye on all three of them."

"I don't know about Jade but Sapphire and Diamond could use an extra pair of eyes on them," they both chuckle.

"I'm going to go and let you get back to it. Is there anything else that I can do for you right now?"

"No, love, I've got it from here."

Love, huh? I'll show you love. "Ok then, see you in a little bit," Taji chimes as she walks out the room blushing.

She runs back downstairs and all three of them just stare.

"Ummm, you wanna tell us what you and our brother were up there doing in that room?" Diamond questions.

"And with the door close no less," Sapphire mutters.

"Hey, hey, y'all, calm ya tits. Your brother just wanted to know if I had any bad history with anyone. He needed information from me that none of you all would know. That's it and that's all. You know that's my first time truly meeting him. I saw him once a long time ago at a BBQ but I do not remember him being that damn fine. I mean damn, he is gorgeous."

"Taji, I know you aren't trying to add my brother to your damn roster?"

"I told you that my roster was closed, Jade."

"Yeah, you did but I know you and I saw the way that you were looking at him."

"Bitch, I've got eyes. He's fine and he made my cat jump a little bit but nothing major," Taji giggles.

"Ewwww bitch, that is our brother. We don't want to hear that shit. He will always be nerdy ass over-protective Onyx to us," Sapphire asserts.

"I can see how you don't see it. He's your brother. You're not supposed to but trust me, that negro is fine as wine and top tier in my opinion. Please trust me. I know men and he is not your ordinary type of guy. He is prime beef baybeee."

"Can we please change the subject? I think that I'm getting sick on the stomach," Jade quips.

"Damn bestie. The thought of me and your brother makes you sick on the stomach? That's disappointing to hear."

"Chile, it's not about you. He's my brother and I don't want to think of him any other way. Plus, I think that the syrup got me again."

"Go on, shitty booty, and handle that. We don't wanna smell you."

Taji hears the door open from upstairs and watches in awe as he descends down the stairs. *Dammit, he's fine. He makes my nipples perk up just looking at him.* Taji clears her throat and asks, "So Onyx, were you able to find anything?"

"Actually, yes, we've already got some feedback. We know that whoever it is uses a system that generates a new number every time the phone is dialed or text. We just have to find out what system that's being used and we can request the data on where the calls are originated from."

"That's good to know. How long does something like that take?"

"Not long. I should know more by the time the day ends."

"Now that we have that out of the way, can we please have our brother back?" Sapphire says in a snarky tone.

"Yes, you may and again, I'm sorry y'all. This whole thing just has me feeling super uneasy and I just want it to be over with. I'm going to head out for a little bit anyway. I have some things to do. That way you will have your brother all to yourself. Which is what you want, I'm sure."

Taji tiptoes over to Onyx, pulls him close, grabs him around his neck, and whispers, "Thank you again for everything. You just don't know how much this means to me." She murmurs as her pussy begins to grow slippery as she embraces him.

"You're welcome, Taji, you don't have to keep thanking me. You are my sister's best friend and she speaks highly of you. I also know that you two were joined at the hip in college. She tells me that you two have always been there for each other and she doesn't know what she would have done if it weren't for you. So I want to thank you, Taji, for making sure that she's good and safe and for taking her in," Onyx affirms as he smiles at Taji and sits back on the sofa.

"Ok, I'm going to skedaddle for a while so I will see you all later."

"Oh, Taji, are you sure that you want to leave right now? Especially considering all that is going on. I would feel better if you stayed for a little while longer. At least until we figure out where these phone calls and texts are originating from. I mean, what if this person is across the street somewhere? It is a possibility that they are watching you and will probably follow you at some point. That's if they haven't followed you already."

"You may have a point, Onyx. Not to mention that you still have my phone. I guess that I will go back up to my room and just chill out until we get some info. You all enjoy yourself and I'll be out of your hair until further notice," Taji states.

CHAPTER 25

I've Got You

Taji treks back up the stairs, feeling a little bit lighter and a lotta bit hornier. Onyx is the type of man that she feels safe with. I mean, he's the FBI, how could she not? She feels like he has things under control, which is foreign to her because Taji is usually in control of every aspect of her life. This situation shows her that sometimes you have to step back and allow others to take over. Onyx did just that and she is completely turned on.

As she arrives at her bedroom door, she gazes down over the living room and admires the hugs and smiles that are being shared by siblings. She closes the door, locks it, and lies across the sofa. Still thinking about the embrace between Onyx and herself, she finds her hands sliding down to penetrate her slippery spot. The skirt that she has on provides her with easy access so that nothing is in her way. Not even panties. She glides her fingers in and out as her sweet spot throbs for more. Taji gets up and reaches into the nightstand for her nine-inch dildo.

If it doesn't put her fire out, nothing will. She lies across the bed this time. She sucks the dildo to add a little moisture before plunging it deep into her pussy. She winces from the pleasure it causes. She then finds her breasts with her other hand and twiddles her nipples, which were already erect and longing to be touch. She tries to quiet herself because she does not want them to know what is taking place in this room.

She continues to thrust the dildo in and out her pussy until that tingle arrives. She's so aroused and doesn't want it to end just yet. She reaches back into the drawer to find her ten inch dildo with the suction cup attached.

She slaps it on the wall and lines her slit up with it perfectly. Taking the cream from her pussy, she slides a little on the dildo and backs into it until she reaches the bottom of her box. Taji rocks and fucks the dildo like a savage. Imagining Onyx sliding his member in and out until she shrieks. Her pussy quakes and thumps from the gratification. She gives her clit some attention and within seconds, she orgasms so hard that her pelvic floor catches a cramp.

She gently leans forward until the huge ten-inch dick

flops out her pussy. *Satisfied* doesn't even describe what she's feeling right now. She removes the dicks from the wall and bed and takes them into the bathroom to clean and dry them. Once she's done, she puts them back in their respective places and flops down on the bed. Thrilled and tired from her session, a nap is sure to follow.

Taji is awakened by light taps on her bedroom door.

"Come in," she chirps.

"Oh, hey, Taji... damn, girl. This bedroom is nice," Onyx states as he looks around. "Anyway, nothing crazy is going on right now but you did get a text message from Chosen. Here, take a look at it."

> Chosen: So this is how you are going to handle me? I haven't heard a peep from you all day. I need to know what the deal is. I'll be at home all day so please pull up. Either way it goes, we need to talk.

"Now, I know that you told me that this guy wants you to be with him. Do you plan on going to him?"

"Yep, that is where I was headed to earlier. I wanted to let him down in person. Some things just aren't meant for text messages. Even though that's how he did me. I'm always going to be the bigger person."

"If you are going to his home, I would prefer that you not go alone. I will come with you."

"Onyx, you don't have to do that. I can handle Chosen. He is as gentle as they come. I truly don't think that he wants to harm me in any way. He just wants to know where my mind is at."

"This may be true, Taji, but that is not a risk that you should be willing to take. I'm a man and I can tell you that there is nothing as fragile as a male's ego. Once that ego is bruised, men can often turn into someone different. I've seen it too many times."

"Now you've got me not wanting to go at all."

"No, I think that you definitely owe it to him to break it off in person. I just don't recommend you doing so alone."

"So, you are willing to come with me forreal?"

"Yes, I am. I'm ready when you are."

"Oh, ok then, Mr. Onyx, you are about that action I see."

"Girl, my sister should have told you about me. I don't play about my loved ones."

"But you just met me."

"And if my sister has been rocking with you this long, then you can't be a bad person. Jade is a sweetheart and the baby of the family. The only sister that I have that thinks first and acts last. You know the other two are all gas no breaks. Jade is logical. If she's kept you around this long and has nothing bad to say, that means that you are a good person."

"So what does that say for Teef?"

"That's a different story." They both chuckle.

"So how are we going to do this? Are you going to ride with me or are you going to trail me?"

"I think it is best if I drive my own vehicle. Just give me the address and I'll follow you and sit in front of the house until you come out."

"OK, that works for me. Before we leave, I just want to say thank you again. Also, if I am not out in 20 minutes, then something is wrong. I'm not long-winded at all. I'm going to say what I have to say and bounce."

"OK, I got you."

"I hate to take you away from your sisters, though. I don't want them to be mad at me."

"They will be all right. This shouldn't take long. When we return, I'm going to take you all out for a nice dinner if that's OK with you."

"Hell yeah, it's OK, I'm never going to turn down free food with a fine ass man. You can bet your life on that."

He laughs, "Taji, you are a mess. I'll be downstairs when you get ready and so you don't have to, I'll go ahead and explain to them what's going on."

"Thank you because I don't need them pissed at me."

Taji gives Onyx Chosen's address, and they take off.

Once she arrives, she hops out of her vehicle and winks at Onyx as she approaches the door.

CHAPTER 26

The Male Ego

C hosen lets her in and Taji stands in the foyer.

"Well, well, well. I wasn't sure if I was going to hear from you today or not. You had me worried for a minute. Come on in and relax. Don't forget to take your shoes off."

"No, I'm not here to stay. I only came by to tell you that I've made my decision. I think that it is best if we go our separate ways so that you can find what you are looking for. You were right in a lot of ways. I want what I want when I want it. I often only think about myself. Maybe I am just not meant for serious relationships and I'm OK with that. You should be OK with it as well. You are a great man, Chosen, and you deserve someone who is willing to give you what you desire. I'm just not that person."

"You mean to tell me that you drove your ass all the way out here to tell me that *it's over?* Is that what you are saying, Taji? You made me waste two years of my life on your ass just to tell me that you don't want or will never want the things that I do. You are a selfish ass bitch."

"I know that you know me well enough to know that I don't play that name calling shit. It is perfectly OK for you to be upset, but I need you to keep your cool."

"Taji, you don't control me and you damn sure can't control how I respond to disrespect. Seriously, who the fuck do you think you are?"

"What do you mean by disrespect? I said nothing disrespectful. You called me a bitch and I just told you that it was uncalled for and to keep your cool. There was no disrespect involved on my end, just on yours."

"You know what, Chosen? I'm not doing this with you. Like I said, have a great life. I'm out."

As Taji turns around to leave, Chosen grabs her by the back of the neck and slams her head against the wall. He then picks her up and throws her to the couch, causing the blinds to collapse. As Onyx scrolls on his phone, he hears the commotion coming from the house. He looks up and notices that he can now see in straight through the window. He sees a man pacing back and forth but doesn't see Taji anywhere. That's enough for him to pounce. He calls the police and gives them Chosen's address, then he races to the front door and attempts to open it. It is locked. He kicks the door in and there lies Taji on the couch, unconscious.

"Who the fuck are you and what are you doing in my house?"

"Never mind who the fuck I am. Why would you put your hands on her like that? Man, she was trying to let you down easy."

"Like I said, who the fuck are you?" Chosen says as he swings at Onyx. Onyx ducks and comes up with an upper cut. They began fighting, knocking over the entry table and even putting a hole in the wall. Chosen is strong, but he is no match for Onyx. Chosen is behaving like a rabid pitbull and Onyx is forced to knock him out. He does so with one solid punch to the temple.

Taji comes to just in time to see Chosen drop to the floor.

"What the fuck just happened, Onyx?"

"I'm not sure what happened with you, but all I know is when I walked through the door, you were lying unconscious on the couch. I tried to subdue him, but he was very irate so I had to knock him out."

"Damn, you knocked him out? Chosen is a pretty big dude. You must really know some shit to knock a big bastard like him out. I still can't believe that motherfucker put his hands on me."

"I told you that men's egos were fragile. Are you OK? We should get you to the hospital and have you checked out."

"No, my head hurts a little, but I'm good. It's no need for all of that. Just help me up."

Onyx helps Taji to her feet, walks her outside, and sits her down in his car. As he enters back into the house, the police arrives. As the police approaches the door, Onyx holds up his badge and explains to them what happened. Chosen is promptly arrested and booked into the Clayton county jail.

Onyx doesn't feel comfortable with Taji driving so they leave her car and return to her house. He takes her keys and opens the door, grabbing her hand and guiding her inside.

Jade and her sisters are in the living room and can clearly see that something is wrong.

"What is going on? Somebody tell me what the fuck is happening," Jade demands.

"My head hurts so I'll let Onyx tell you what happened. I'm going to go upstairs and lie down."

"No, Taji, you cannot do that. I can't let you lie down at least for a couple of hours. There is a possibility that you may have a concussion and since you refused to go to the hospital, we won't know. You have to stay awake so go over there and sit down on the couch next to Jade and let her keep an eye on you," Onyx orders.

Taji walks over to where Jade is, sits down, and lies on her shoulder. Jade is stunned.

"Onyx, you are truly going to have to tell us what happened because my friend that I've known for 15 years has never followed orders from any man. You tell her to go sit down and she does. She definitely must've hit her head because I've never seen her submit to a man so fast."

Onyx begins explaining what happens and they are all in shock. Jade gets up and prepares an ice pack for Taji. Sapphire and Diamond get her favorite blanket and drapes it across her lap.

Onyx receives a phone call and excuses himself. While he is taking care of whatever business he has, Jade comforts and talks to Taji in an attempt to prevent her from sleeping.

"I'm sorry that this happened to you. You were just trying to let him go find what he feels he needs, and he couldn't take it. The only thing he wanted to hear was, *yes Chosen, I'll do whatever you want.* That's on him because his ass should have known better."

"Let me change the subject for a second. Don't think that I haven't noticed that you are sweet on my brother, and I can honestly say that I don't blame you. He is such a great guy. However, I'm telling you now as his little sister and your best friend, he will not be on any roster that you have. I want you to leave my brother alone if you can't love him the way he deserves."

"Onyx is not roster material. He doesn't deserve a spot. He deserves *the* spot. I love you, Taji, but if you can't give him your all, then I want you to leave him the fuck alone. I mean this in the nicest way possible."

"Whoa, whoa, whoa! I didn't say that I was sweet on anybody. He is a very nice guy, but I'm not focused on adding anybody to my roster. Besides, bitch, this nigga Chosen smashed my head into a fucking wall. I don't wanna hear this shit right now. I'm not focused on your brother. I'm focused on trying to figure out who the fuck this is watching and stalking us. That's all."

"Try that shit with someone else. I know you and I know when you are interested in somebody. You get a twinkle in your eye whenever they come around. I know you, Taji. You don't have to lie to me. It's OK, I'm just telling you that my brother will not be played with. Now there are a lot of things that I mess around with, but my family is not one of them. Especially him and I'm sure that my sisters feel the same way.

"OK OK. I hear you. Anyway, I'm hungry. That bacon wasn't enough. What else do we have here to eat?"

"Onyx is taking us out to dinner. Are you well enough to come?" Diamond asks.

"Hell yes. You all are not about to leave and eat without me. Somebody hand me an ibuprofen. I'm hungry as a hostage. Did he say where he was going to take us? If he doesn't know, there are a couple of places that I can recommend."

Onyx descends the stairs with a troubled look upon his face. Heading straight towards Jade, he kneels down in front of her and grabs her hand.

"I'm so sorry, baby sister, but I have some bad news. Reggie is dead. He was murdered before day this morning. They found his body in a motel room on the west end."

CHAPTER 27

Crime of Passion

"Wait, wait. What did you just say? Did you say that my husband is *dead*? Is that what you said, Onyx? How? What happened?" Jade questions as tears begin to form in her eyes.

"What happened isn't really important right now, Jade. You just need to know that he's gone," Onyx quips.

"No, you don't get to tell me that *my husband* is **fucking dead** and not tell me what happened to him. What the fuck happened to my husband?"

"Jade, I don't think that is appropriate that I say it in front of everyone."

"Fuck the formalities, Onyx. Everyone in this house is family. Everyone in this house knows me and my situation. There are no secrets, so tell me what happened to him."

"He was shot in the head by his lover's wife. She had her husband's location and she followed him to the motel. The housekeeper let her in and she found them in the act. She killed both of them and then waited for the police to get there. She is in custody as we speak. I'm so sorry, baby girl. The homicide detectives were on their way over to let you know. I asked them to let me tell you."

"So let me get this straight. *My* husband was with another *man* in a hotel. *His wife* caught them in the act and shot them **both** dead?"

"Yes, Jade. That sums it up."

Jade scoots back on the sofa, crosses her hands, and rests them on her lap. Her tears dry up faster than a raindrop in 100 degree weather. She doesn't utter a word. Diamond, Sapphire, and Onyx all go over to comfort her, but she pushes everyone away.

"No, I'm good, y'all. There is no need to fret over me. I'm fine. I know that you were going to take us out to dinner, Onyx. I think it will probably be best if we do that another day. However, I am still hungry so is it possible that we call in our orders for pick up? Would you mind going to get it?"

"Jade, are you serious right now? Onyx just told you that your husband was dead and you're talking about food," Sapphire states.

"Well, yeah. We've got to eat. You want me to be sad?

You want me to be hurt? Well, I would probably be both of those things if Onyx was telling me that my husband died in a car accident or hell even a random robbery. That isn't the case though, now is it? My husband was shot and killed because he was fucking someone else's husband and got caught. Not only was he cheating on me, he was cheating on me with *a man*, not just a man but *a married* man, so no. He gets no sympathy from me. I will bury him and do my wifely duties but sad I will not be. Pissed off, yes but sad, no. Now I'm thinking, Longhorns or Texas Roadhouse for dinner. What about y'all?"

"Jade, they want you to come down and identify the body," Onyx says in a somber tone.

"Nope, I will not. Get somebody else to do it. Tell them that I have family in town and that I'm busy. I do not get to see you all very often, so I'd rather be here with you all right now."

"They would like a family member to identify the body," he advises.

"Ok, I'm not the only family member in this town. Call his mama or his brother. In their eyes, he could do no wrong so let them do it because I'm not. I don't want to see him ever again. Not in a motel, a body bag, a casket, an urn, not even on a fucking obituary. Do you understand?"

"Okay. I will let them know that you will not be

coming down and to contact someone else," Onyx announces.

"Thank you. Now, is anybody going to place an order? I'm so hungry that I'm about to disappear."

At this point, no one knows what to say or do so they continue as if nothing happened. Diamond grabs her phone and googles the number to Longhorns. She asks everyone what they would like, then places the order. Onyx agrees to slide through and pick it up.

Everyone in the house went from watching Taji to make sure that she's ok to watching Jade. Waiting for her to show some signs of sadness or grief, but she gives them nothing.

Taji watches her closely as ever. She completely agrees with everything Jade said, but the fact that Jade is the one that said it throws her off. She's always known Jade to be soft hearted, gentle, caring, and kind. She's never shown coldness this way but it just proves what a detriment Reggie was to her mental health. She's rigid, removed, numb. Hurt and anguish has done that to her.

Jade always told Taji that no matter what happens, you should always remain a lady and take the highroad. Taji knows that deep down inside, Jade is hurt but her anger won't let her show it. Taji certainly won't press her to feel anything that she doesn't want to.

"Jade, is there anything you need from us? Like, is there anything that we can do?" Sapphire queries.

"As a matter of fact it is. I would love it if you two extend this weekend for a few more days. I will pay you what you are missing in wages. I am going to need some help."

"Ok, we can do that. We just need to make a few phone calls to our bosses. What are you going to need help with?" Diamond asks.

"I want one of you to go down there tomorrow with me to make the funeral arrangements. You have my full permission to put him away but make sure that you select the cheapest rate. I'll be in the car until it's time to sign the paperwork. Once that is done, I will return back to my home and start getting rid of his things. That is what I need your help with. I want every single thing that belongs to Reggie out of *my* house."

"I know that you all think that I'm going crazy, but I am not. I know exactly what I am saying and why I'm saying it. For years, I have dealt with all kinds of shit from him. Every other night, I was worried about where he was, who he was with, what he was doing, what time he would come home. Night after night, I worried."

"I am at peace because I don't have to worry anymore about where he is. I know for sure. I am at peace because I don't have to go through a terrible divorce, split my assets, or worry about what he would try and take from me. I am also at peace because I am the beneficiary of a very sizable insurance policy. A couple of them actually. So, I am good in every sense of the word. I started grieving for my husband and my marriage a long time ago. Way before today."

"I know that you all love me and no matter what I say, you will worry. I promise that you don't have to. I'm good. You don't have to worry about my mental health either because if I need counseling, I will get it."

"Now, if it is OK with all of you all, let's not bring his name up anymore. Let's enjoy our time together. Onyx, I'm sure that the food is ready. Will you go ahead and pick it up?"

"Yes, I'm getting ready to head out now. Does anyone need anything else while I'm out?"

"Yes, can you stop by the liquor store and get us a few bottles of champagne, please, Onyx?" Jade requests.

"Champagne? Jade, really?" Onyx sneers.

"Yes, I love champagne. Don't you?"

"Jade, I know that you are hurting, but celebrating your husband's death is really something that you shouldn't be doing."

"See Onyx, big brother, you've got it all wrong. I'm not celebrating his death. I'm celebrating my life." Jade maintains. "Please pick a good brand, too. Those cheap brands give me the bubble guts."

"Ok Jade, I'll get your champagne. Does anyone else want anything?"

"Oh Onyx, I have a bar full of liquor, so I don't need anything, but I would like a Goody Powder if you can find one. This ibuprofen hasn't done anything. With all of the shit that has gone on today, my blood pressure is probably sky high," Taji quips.

"Ok, I've gotten everybody's order so I'm about to head out. I will see y'all in a little bit," he remarks as he leaves out the front door.

CHAPTER 28

Standing on Business

J ade's phone begins ringing off the hook. Everyone is calling to extend their condolences, and she doesn't care to speak to any of them. She lets all the calls go to voicemail besides his mother. When she calls, Jade answers.

"Hello, Mrs. Baker. What can I do for you?"

"You can get down to that damn office and identify my boy's body. That's what the fuck you can do for me," she says while crying and yelling.

"No ma'am, I cannot but you or Dominic are welcome to. Listen, I will never be disrespectful to you because I was raised better than that. But, you need to know that you son was not the angel that you thought he was. I don't owe him anything."

"What do you mean, Jade? He is your damn husband.

It's your responsibility to put him away in a decent manner. He would do the same for you."

"Are you sure about that, Mrs. Baker? The way that he treated me up until his death wasn't indicative of someone that gave a damn about his wife. Your son cheated on me time and time again. He ignored me and even gave me a damn disease. So tell me again how he would have done the same for me? Here's what I suggest. You all are more than welcome to do whatever you like with his body. You can even have another funeral for him if you want. I'm telling you now, I'm getting the cheapest plan. A pine box if they have it. He broke our covenant a long time ago so I don't owe him *shit*."

"Jade, I never knew that you were such a low-down dirty bitch."

"I wasn't but you have your son to thank for that. He did this to me. I was practically an angel before he got ahold of me. Don't worry. I'm going to work on myself and get back to me but as for now, I will wear the title of a low-down bitch with pride. Let's see how jovial you would be if your husband was caught fucking another man in a seedy ass hotel! Let's see if you would be as forgiving. Now goodbye."

Jade hangs up the phone and heads into the kitchen to fix herself a drink. While she mixes the Hennessy and Coke she looks up and realizes that the whole house is watching her.

"Can y'all not do that? Over there staring at me like I'm some kind of exhibit."

"We don't mean to. It's just that we've never seen you like this. I kinda like this Jade. This Jade stands on business," Sapphire boasts. "I mean, shit. If we are keeping it real, she said nothing wrong. That nigga wasn't no angel and was doing our good sis wrong. Nobody is about to cry over his ass. I sure the fuck won't."

"So are we still going to have game night tonight? After we eat dinner, we can all go to my house. Taji, I will be out of your hair by nightfall. I'm going home. Hey, y'all," she yells. "Pack your things. We are going home."

"Wait, Jade. You all don't have to leave. You can stay here. At least for a few more days."

"Taji, are you crazy? I have my own empty house to go to. Why would I stay here? Don't get me wrong. I love and appreciate you for everything but it's time for me to be back in my own space."

"All that shit that was going on should stop. The culprit is dead. I think that you can rest easy, Taji. At least I hope so. If not, you can come over to my house and stay with me for awhile."

Onyx trucks through the front door with four big bags

full of food and champagne. Putting the bags down in the kitchen, he anxiously tells Taji to get up and meet him outback on the deck. With her icepack in tow, she hoists herself off the couch and follows Onyx out the backdoor. He grabs her hand and they walk about one hundred feet away from the house and he pulls out her phone.

"As soon as I pulled away from the house, a message came through on your phone. I think that it's safe to say that Reggie isn't involved. It seems as if you have a certified stalker on your hands. Check it out, look what he sent."

> Unknown number: What happened to your whore ass? One of those niggas probably found out that you were fucking around on him and beat you like the whore you are. Who is that simp ass nigga that you've got laying up in your house now? Taji, I tell you. You never learn do you.

"Once that message came through, I sent one back, acting like you. Telling him to go to hell and if he were really about that action that he would show up while everyone was here. Not to wait until everyone was gone. He told me that in due time that I would know who he was and then he sent a picture. Do you recognize this picture, Taji?"

On her phone was a picture of Taji laying diagonally

across the bed with her negligee on. She covers her mouth out of disbelief.

"Oh my God, Onyx. He has a camera hidden somewhere in my room. That is what I was wearing the night before your sisters came. That is scary, Onyx. I had my camera man, Ajani, come and do a sweep the day that we returned home. Jade's room had been rummaged through, so I called him. He didn't find anything. Whoever it is must have broken in again after he left and installed it. Here I was thinking that it was someone watching Jade and they are watching *me*. What do I do, Onyx?"

"You just continue doing what you always do. Be cool. I've got my entire tech team on it and we will figure it out. This is what we do. They advised me that the phone calls were pinging off the same tower that your phone pings off. He's super close. Maybe even across the street. Do you know your neighbors?"

"Not really, I'm more of a wave and go in my house type of person. I don't know any of them by name."

"From the information that they have gathered, there are 4 vacant houses on this street. He's probably watching you from one of those. They also advised that there is another source tapped into the cameras that you already have installed."

"This could also be another way that he is able to keep

tabs on who is coming and going. Don't worry. At some point during the day, I'll go up there to find and disable the camera in the bedroom. It shouldn't be too hard to find considering the angles. Listen, these things rarely end pretty. You are going to have to watch your back fiercely and keep your head on a swivel at all times. I don't want you to let the worry consume you though. I've got your back."

"I don't know how much you can have my back when you're not here. Jade is ready to go home. She just told your sisters to pack their stuff."

"I'm my own man and Jade doesn't tell me what to do. I'm going to stay here with you and make sure that this thing is handled. You can't ask for my help and not expect me to finish what I started. Jade and I will have plenty of time to spend together. I'm here for good, remember? Anyhow, back to this. At some point, he's going to feel comfortable showing himself. He will try you and that is when we will bring him down. It's honestly a good thing that they are leaving. Less collateral damage and with everyone gone, he's going to think that he's got you all alone. I've got a plan for all of this, Jade. Are you down?"

"Hell yes, I am, but lets go back inside and eat first. Then we will talk about it."

"Ok but we cannot talk about anything in the house.

We don't know where the cameras are installed or if it were any bugs left."

"Understood," Taji concedes. "I won't say anything," she mutters as she opens the back door leading into her home.

CHAPTER 29

Go Ahead and Go

They stroll back into the house and all eyes are directed at them. Taji searches through the bag to find the order with her name on it.

"Umm, why are you two being so secretive? Onyx, are you not going to let us know what is going on? If Reggie was the one doing it, then nothing else should happen."

"Diamond, I know that you want to know what's going on and you will. Just not right now. Just know that we are working on resolving the problem."

"I hate when you do that fancy ass, proper, FBI talk, Onyx. Just tell us what's going on man," Diamond gripes.

"That's the thing, Diamond. He can't. He told you that he will tell you when he's able so please leave it at that. A lot of shit has happened today and is currently happening, but it is not safe for us to share it with you right now. So for the sake of my sanity, can you please just leave it alone? Nobody is keeping secrets from you. Just know that it is being worked out."

"Onyx, after everyone finishes eating, we are going to pack up and head over to my house," Jade quips. "Taji, are you coming, too? You should, you don't have anything else going on. I don't expect you to participate because I know that you have a headache. I just want my best friend to be there with me."

Taji looks at Onyx to gauge what she should do, he nods his head *yes*.

"Ok, I'll come over. You are right. I don't have shit else going on but a headache, so I'll be there. Oh, can someone go get my car from Chosen's house? Whoever volunteers, I'll pay for your Uber and give you $100.00 for your trouble."

Sapphire raises her hand. "I'll go as soon as I finish eating. I'm not turning down that good money."

"Thank you, Sapphire. The key is on the hook next to the garage door. It's the one with the BMW fob of course and please don't be driving my shit all crazy. Jade told me about all those tickets that you have."

"Jade knows that she runs her damn mouth too much," Sapphire chirps as she continues devouring her steak and rolling her eyes at Jade..

"Onyx, can you hand me my phone for a minute? Let

me go ahead and call her an Uber. They should be here by the time she's done stuffing her face."

"Is everyone just about done eating? I'm ready to go home. I miss my house so much. I can't wait to get home and have Maria deep clean the house. I'm going to stop at HomeGoods on my way home from the funeral home tomorrow and buy new sheets and shit. There is no telling what was going on in that house."

"Jade, please don't piss me off and stop rushing people. If you are in such a hurry to go, just go ahead and go home. When Sapphire returns with my car, we will head over there."

"Good, I'm gonna take my food and champagne and go. Taji, thank you again for everything and I will come by tomorrow to get my things. I will also clean the room and leave it just like I found it. Ok, bookie?" she says as she bends down and kisses Taji on her cheek. "See y'all in a little bit," Jade mumbles as she skips out the door.

"Uh huh, whatever, Jade. Onyx, please tell me that you didn't forget my Goody Powder?"

"I didn't. It should be in one of those bags. It's in a small brown paper sack."

"Found it. Thank you so much," she says as she pours the powder on her tongue. "I don't think anything exists like a Goody Powder. This will knock your headache out within 10 minutes. My dad used to take them all the time for hangovers."

"Taji, is your father still living? I've heard Jade talk about your mother before, but nothing about your father."

"According to my towns people, my father disappeared when I was about 14, so no. He is no longer in the picture."

"Damn, I'm so sorry to hear that. That must've been tough to lose your father is such a young age?"

"I lost him long before that. I was nine when he ran off with his side bitch. That was my last time seeing him. The word on the street back home was that he is dead but I've never seen a body nor have I heard of one being found. For all I know, his ass is still out there somewhere."

"Have you or your mother ever done a search for him, Taji?"

"Nope, at least I haven't. I don't know what my mother has done."

"Well, maybe one day I can look into it for you and see what we can find."

"No, I'm good. It's OK to let sleeping dogs lie."

"I'm going to say it because no one has but I know that you all have to be thinking it. I'm really worried about my girl. She's taking this shit a little too well." Taji admits.

"I know, right?" Diamond chuckles. "It's damn near

scary. I knew that she was sick and tired of that nigga and was ready to divorce him, but my sister seems happy as fuck to be rid of him. I mean, talking about deep cleaning and getting rid of all of his shit. I guess what they say is true. When a woman is fed up and loses respect for you, there is no going back."

"Sapphire, your Uber is outside," Taji announces.

Sapphire grabs the key fob and darts out the door, but she comes right back in.

"Bitch, how are you going to send me somewhere and not tell me the man's address?"

"Because I already keyed it in when I booked the Uber. The Uber driver knows where you are going, but just in case, it's 8392 Havana's Way."

"You know what? I don't want you going alone, so I will go with you," Diamond asserts.

"Well, hurry up. The lady is out here waiting on us." Sapphire urges as they both exit the front door.

CHAPTER 30

Beautifully Broken

"Oh Lord, they have left us alone. Now they are going to be looking all googly eyed when they get back. Those girls are protective as hell about you, Onyx. They do realize that you are a grown ass man, don't they?"

"Doesn't seem like it, does it? I'm the oldest. You would think that they would have learned to fall back by now, but nope. Not them," he laughs.

"I think it's sweet though. How protective they are of you. It's cute."

"Yeah, it is, I'm the same way about them."

"Jade used to brag on you heavy when her and I first met. My brother is this, my brother is that. Now I can completely understand why. You are a sweet guy. Especially for coming in and taking charge like you have. I appreciate that."

"And you seem like a good woman. That man putting his hands on you was crazy though. You must have really hurt his feeling. I kept thinking, *damn, she said this was a good dude.* He sure didn't seem like a good dude to me. He seemed like a madman. Taji, you've gotta tell me what you are doing to these brothers to make them crash out over your ass like that."

"I'm not doing anything, Onyx. Especially to be getting stalked and beat up. They can have that shit. I don't play that putting your hands on me kind of shit. I'm already raised and I am who I'm going to be. Hitting me isn't going to make me change. Plus, I don't switch up on people. What you see is what you get with me and I'm not going to promise anything that I can't deliver."

"Taji, let me ask you this and be honest. Although I have a feeling that you won't lie to me, why haven't you settled down for real? You've got this big ass nice house, a cute little dog running around here. You seem successful although, no offense, I don't know what you do. You've got a couple of nice rides. You seem to have everything but love and someone to share it with. You mean to tell me that you don't ever want that?"

"Boy, you and your sister are more alike than you

know. She asks me the same questions all the time. Like I said before, that love shit is overrated. Love will get you hurt. Notice I said *will*, not can. It's a certainty in my eyes. I've been through a lot, Onyx. Men haven't given me many reasons to trust them so I don't and I don't think that I ever will. I mean, I thought Chosen was a good guy and look at how that turned out. The one time he doesn't get his way he beats me up. That shit is not cool. I'm not about to sit around and wait for somebody to switch up on me."

"You have got to know that all men are not the same, Taji. I can tell that you've been hurt but trust me when I tell you that there are some great guys out here. And I really mean great guys. Not pretending to be great like Chosen. Some of us can be trusted and if that is honestly how you feel, that's a sad take on love. I'd give anything to have someone to do life with. That's the reason why I took this job here. I'm getting older. It's time to settle down and lie down some roots. I was tired of being on the west coast all by myself. I'm a good old country boy with country boy values and that wasn't appreciated in Cali. Women out there looked at it as if I was corny. I'm hoping that I have better luck here."

"Onyx, as fine as you are, I doubt very seriously if you will have a problem finding someone. These women are going to see you and yolk you right up."

"Thanks for the compliment but I don't know about

all that. Besides, I'm looking for something special. I don't want what everyone else is getting or has had. In other words, I don't want just *someone* but *the one*."

"Well, the pickings are slim in ATL. Everybody knows everybody and they all run in the same circle. I want to give you some tips."

"No disrespect, Taji, but I don't need any tips. I just need the right woman. I'm not in a rush and when God places her in front of me, I'll know. I've prayed for her. I also prayed that God builds me up to be the man that I need to be for her. I've prayed for discernment. When the time comes, I'll be right where I need to be. Ya dig?"

"Dug," Taji laughs. "That's beautiful, Onyx."

"What's beautiful?"

"Your mindset. The fact that you prayed to God to prepare you and ready you to receive His blessing. That's deep. Having a wife is indeed a blessing and I hope you truly find her. When you do, she should know that she's a lucky, oh wait, I mean a "blessed" woman. On that note, I'm going to go freshen up before we head over to Jade's house. Sapphire should be back soon."

"Before you go off and do that, would you mind showing me where you keep your tool set? I'm gonna go up there in the room and find the camera and disable it."

"Sure, it's in the garage on the other side of the Lamborghini."

After Onyx finishes finding and removing the camera, Taji gets up and makes a beeline straight to her bedroom. Looking down, she realizes that her palms are sweaty, and her heart is beating out of her chest. Onyx explaining his thought process has her swooning and rethinking her whole life. She also thinks about her best friend's words. "Leave my brother alone if you can't love him properly."

Taji knows that she has issues and needs to handle them. She starts to think that maybe if she heals the broken pieces of herself, she may have a chance at loving a deserving man correctly.

The abuse that she has experienced in her past has led her to believe that no man can be trusted. She wonders if maybe, just maybe, she's wrong. For her sake, she wants to be. She wants to heal but doesn't have any faith in the process. Her mind tells her that even that beautiful, kind, caring man downstairs can't be trusted but her heart tells her differently. However, she doesn't trust her own heart.

All this thinking and feeling overwhelms her. She attempts to push the conversation that she and Onyx had out of her mind, but it's painfully obvious that she feels safe and comforted when Onyx is near. Speaking to him intimately makes her grasp the reality that she may indeed be *the problem*. It's as if accountability jumped up and slapped her in the face. "***I'm** the problem. **I'm** the one that's* *broken and it's my responsibility to fix me.*" She gripes to herself.

I need to be a better person. It starts with me. Her head begins to ache. She reaches up and touches the sore spot on her head. It's an awful reminder of what happens when feelings are involved, and shit goes terribly wrong. She hates that it came to that with Chosen but in retrospect, she understands his anger but not the abuse.

She stands in front of the mirror and takes a good look at herself. A beautifully broken woman stares back at her. For the first time in her life, she doesn't like what she sees. On the surface is beauty, charm, confidence, and whit. All the things that have gotten her everything she wants. Beneath the surface is anger, madness, hatred, and fear, which prevents her from getting the thing that she needs. Healing.

She's startled when Onyx darkens her bedroom door.

"Taji, I'm sorry. I didn't mean to scare you, but I've been calling you for the last couple of minutes. When you didn't answer, I got worried and ran up here. Are you about ready to head over to Jade's house? Sapphire and Diamond are back and we are all packed up and ready to go."

"Yes, I'm ready. Just let me grab my purse and jacket and we can bounce. You are driving, right? I know you all don't trust me to drive to the mailbox right now," Taji chirps.

"And you would be absolutely correct. I will do the driving. We will be down here waiting on you."

"I'm coming." Taji says as she double checks her purse for her gun and the extra magazines. She looks around her room and wonders where the camera that's been watching her for Lord knows how long was placed, wondering if whomever it is will continue rummaging through her things while she's away. Or if they will spray her favorite perfume to get a whiff of what she smells like daily. She wonders if they will play with Bella while she's gone. The thought of her home being violated in such a way is too real. A wave of anger hovers over her like a drone. *Whoever this muthafucka is, has got to go.*

Taji runs down the stairs and grabs Sapphire's hands to steady herself. She's still feeling a little woozy but doesn't trouble anyone. They've all been troubled enough.

Sapphire throws the keys to Onyx and they load up. Onyx hops in and adjust the seats and mirrors.

"Taji, I don't see how you drive this thing this late at night. The tint is dark as hell."

"That's the point. I don't want anyone to see me coming or to see who I have in my car."

"Mission accomplished then. I'm surprised that you

haven't gotten 10 tickets already," he utters as he speeds away.

They arrive to see Jade sitting out on her wrap around porch, in her pajamas and robe, enjoying a cup of tea. Looking as calm and relaxed as if she didn't just get the news that her husband of eight years was dead.

"I thought that I would have to come back and see what was going on. What took you all so long? Traffic?" Jade questions.

"Yes," Sapphire admits. "I'm not used to driving in this mess but the one thing that I do love is there seems to be no speed limit. The bad thing is that they will run your ass over is you do decide to go slow. I made it back as fast as I could and once I did, we came right over."

"I guess I'm going to have to get used to the traffic, huh?" Onyx quips.

"Why, will you be here for long, big brother?" Jade queries.

"Yes, I was going to wait to tell you all but there is no time like the present. I took another position. I'm here for good."

They all scream with excitement and hurry into the house. Taji is the last to enter. She's taking it slow and easy. She takes three steps into the house before dropping to the floor.

CHAPTER 31

Care For Me

"Taji, Taji.......wake up... please, best friend. Please wake up. Can't nobody else be dying on me today," is what Taji hears as she looks up and peers into Jade's and Onyx's faces.

"What the hell happened?"

"You passed out is what happened. Now Taji, this is just stupid. Why won't you let me take you to the hospital?" Onyx pleads.

"Because I don't need to go to the hospital. I'm fine. I think that I'm just a little dehydrated."

"Now Taji," Jade chirps. "You had a 225 pound man smash your head into the wall and throw you on his couch and you are sitting here telling us that you are dehydrated. Onyx is right. This is so stupid. You are my best friend. I can't lose you, too. You are getting your ass in that BMW and letting Onyx drive you to the hospital. I am no longer asking, I'm *telling*. Now get your apple bottomed ass in that car before I knock you the fuck out again. I've had a long day. Between a fucking stalker, you getting jumped on, and my gay dead husband, enough is enough," Jade yells.

"Okay, okay, just please stop yelling, Jade. I will go. Please, just stop screaming."

"Thank you. Onyx, please pick her up and carry her to her car. Game night has been postponed until further notice," Jade yells as she slips Taji's shoe back onto her feet. "Please call me when you know what's going on, Onyx. Oh, and thank you for taking her stubborn ass. This day has been eventful as hell," she says as she waltzes back into the house and closes the door behind her.

Taji and Onyx arrive at the hospital, and she is seen immediately. Three hours later, Taji is released. Discharged papers are handed to Onyx, citing concussion, low potassium, and dehydration. She is given orders to follow-up with her regular care physician.

"I'm taking you home and I am staying the night as promise. There is no way that I could leave you alone after this. Taji, do you know how bad this could have turned out if you were alone? I don't think that I have to tell you."

"You don't and I'm thankful that you all were there.

I'm just glad that I get to go home to my bed and finally rest."

"When we get there, I'll draw a bath for you if you don't mind. I think that it could really help you. Do you have Epsom salt?"

"I'm a black woman in the south, of course I do." They both chuckle.

"Now that it's just you and me and we are not in my house, what is your plan?"

"I don't want you to worry about that right now. We will talk about that tomorrow. This has been a long ass day and I'm just as tired as you. If not more. I'm going to have to get used to being back on Eastern Standard Time."

They travel about 20 minutes until they reach Taji's home. She tells him to pull into the garage. Onyx gets out and runs around to Taji's side and opens the car door. Grabbing her hand, he helps her to her feet. She wobbles a little as she tries to steady herself. Onyx notices and picks her up and carries her inside the house. Once inside, he helps her to her bedroom, then runs back downstairs to lock and secure all doors and windows. He treks back upstairs and runs Taji's bathwater as promised. Pouring Epsom salt in the water, he asks her where she keeps her pajamas. She points and he promptly picks out a set and lays it across her bed. She is thankful for the care that he is showing her but Taji can't help but think about Chosen.

He used to do this very thing for her and look what an asshole he turned out to be.

Before she overthinks too much and utters a word, she bridles her tongue. This is her first attempt at not lumping all men together. She reminds herself that Onyx is not Chosen and that Onyx has nothing to gain by being there. He is doing this out of the kindness of his heart. She remains thankful that someone is there to care for her in this moment.

"Taji, I do believe that you are all set. I'm going to head down to the bedroom that you have for me and turn in for the night. If you need anything, just holler and I'll be right here." As he turns to leave the bedroom, his phone rings and it's Jade.

"Where in the hell are you two? It's been hours and we haven't heard anything. It's past my bedtime and I am up waiting to see what's wrong with my girl."

"Baby sis, I am so sorry. I meant to call you when they discharged her. She's ok. She has a slight concussion, low potassium, and she was indeed dehydrated. She's good now. She's about to take a bath and lie down."

"Wait," Jade grunts. "Are you over there with her right now?"

"As a matter of fact, I am. She needs somebody here. I know what you went through today, but she went through something tragic as well. Despite your husband dying, you seem completely fine. She is not. You were so damn ready to go home that you didn't think of anybody but yourself. This girl opened her home to you. To us. She was there for you and had your back through it all and I can't believe that you were so quick to leave her. I wasn't going to say shit, but you need to know that you are wrong. I thought that she was your best friend. It wouldn't have hurt you to stay another night. Hell, this is the time when you should be there for one another. So be mad all you want but you should be mad at *yourself*. Now I love you, little sis, and I will see y'all tomorrow. I'm going to bed. Goodnight and goodbye," he says as he hangs up the phone.

As soon as the call ends, another one comes through. Picking up the phone, he places whoever is on the other line on hold.

"Taji, I must take this call. Go ahead and get in the tub and I'll be back in here in a little while to check on you," he mutters as he walks down the hallway.

Taji slowly makes her way to the bathroom and disrobes. She tells Alexa to play her soft girl playlist and she gently slides into the steaming hot water. All at once her troubles seem to disappear. She knows that it's temporary, but she doesn't let it stop her from enjoying it.

She smiles at the thought of Onyx standing up for her the way that he did. Onyx came in handling business and hasn't stopped since he's gotten here. If standing on business was a person, it would surely be him. Onyx comes back to the bedroom door and tells her that he needs to speak with her. She can barely hear him. She tells him to come in. He does and takes a seat on the chaise and waits her for to exit the bathroom.

"Onyx, you can come in here. I'm still in the tub."

He comes to the bathroom door with his eyes closed and tells her that he has more information.

"Good, come in and tell me about it."

"But aren't you still in the tub? I don't want to invade your privacy."

"If I'm telling you to come in then you aren't invading anything. Onyx, I'm not nor have I ever been bashful. You've seen titties and pussy before, right?"

"Ummm, yes," he quips.

"Ok then. It's all pretty much the same. Maybe a different size, color, or smell but it's about the same," Taji giggles.

Onyx opens his eyes and has a seat on the toilet.

"Taji, earlier today, I submitted the first picture of the unsub to my team. They are working on identifying him. The picture that you gave me was clear as day. Since you do not recognize him, I submitted it for facial recognition. Now, some things we do know. Whomever it is, is very tech savvy. He's extremely bold. He likely has an extensive criminal background. Definitely obsessed with you and feels like you owe him something. Can you think of any male suitors that you cut off without closure?"

"Not at this moment, Onyx. To be honest, I can't think of much," Taji says as she grabs the towel and stands up.

Onyx attempts to turn his head and focus on his words, but he cannot. He is mesmerized by her body. Her shape. Her long legs. The way the water glistens on her skin. He looks at Taji and can't help but think, *perfection*.

"Taji, would you like for me to leave while you get dressed?"

"No, what I would like is for you to sleep in here with me tonight. Look, I know that you just met me today but I'm a bit afraid to sleep alone. I promise not to touch you, Onyx. I would just feel safer with you here in the room with me. Would you mind?"

Stuttering, "Umm, ummm... no. I don't mind. I can do that. Would you like for me to sleep on that couch over there or on the chaise?"

"I want you to sleep in the bed. Next to me. That's the only way that I'm going to feel safe. Oh, and my friend lying next to my nightstand will help," she utters as she points to the AK47.

"Ohhh shit, Taji. How come I've never seen that there?"

"I don't know but she's ready. There is also a 45 under

the pillow that you will be sleeping on and a 9mm under mine."

He lifts his T-shirt. Not only revealing rock-hard abs, but also a rock hard dick and a hard piece of steel.

"Damn, are you going to sleep with your gun on you?" she questions as she tries her best not to stare at his enormous dick print.

"Taji, no. I was just showing you that it's pretty much always on me. Bed is seriously the only time that I remove it, and it usually stays right beside me. I'm always strapped."

"Great, looks like we are ready for bed then." Taji says as she throws the decorative pillows to the sofa and slide the cover back. "Onyx, do you prefer to sleep with the tv off or on?"

"It doesn't matter. I can sleep through just about anything."

"Don't sleep too hard. You won't be able to hear if you are dead to the world."

"I'll do my best but I want you to do your best by not putting that big old ass on me. I'm a gentleman and I try to be respectful but I'm still a man. I don't need you knocking me in the head in the middle of the night because my dick got hard. Dicks do that, ya know."

"Onyx, I'm not a little girl. I've got a whole stalker. I'm worried about *his* dick being in the wrong place. Not yours," she says as she grabs her pillow and rolls over on her side.

"See, there you are starting already. I never agreed to be the big spoon. Hold up, let me go in this room and slide on some jogging pants or something. Me and these little basketball shorts are not going to work if you are going to be doing all that. I need some kind of barrier."

"Onyx, no. You don't have to do that. I will be alright. I'm cool. I promise."

"But I'm not. Girl, you keep backing that thang up on me and I'm gonna push forward eventually. I don't want any problems. I'm trying to remain respectful."

"Ok, I'll turn towards you then. Would that be better?"

"Absolutely. Thank you."

"You're welcome," she says as she flips over and stares into his big brown eyes.

Within minutes, Onyx is out for the count. Taji watches as his beautifully chiseled chest rises up and down. She marvels at the thick vein that bulges in his neck with every heartbeat. She follows the traces of his lips with her finger and finds herself inching closer to him. So close that their lips almost touch. There is where she finds comfort and security. There is where she finally finds *peace*.

CHAPTER 32

Like A Rock

Taji wakes up the next morning feeling well rested and rejuvenated. She is so thankful to Onyx for staying the night. As a token of her gratitude, she decides to prepare a nice breakfast for him. She slips on her robe, grabs her phone and pistol, and treks downstairs. She lets Bella out to handle her business, then makes her way to the kitchen to prepare a nice breakfast for Onyx. She quickly places an order to have groceries delivered.

Taji doesn't spare any expenses either. After all, the man has been in Cali for ages. There is no telling when's the last time that he had a home cooked meal. She makes creole shrimp and grits with bacon and andouille sausage, catfish filets, lobster omelets, fresh fruit, and freshly squeezed orange juice. Onyx gets up and treks to his room to prepare for a day with his sisters but the aroma detours him and drags him to the kitchen.

"Girl, what do you have going on down here? It smells good as hell."

"I figured that you could use a home cooked meal. You said that you were on the west coast alone. That most likely meant that you had no one to cook for you so I decided that I would. I want to thank you again for doing all that you have done. I mean seriously, it's special. You sacrificed time with your sisters for little old me and I wanted to show some gratitude."

"Girl, you didn't have to put it down like this but I appreciate it. Ummm, is that creole shrimp and grits?"

"Yes, it is. Would you like some?"

"Yes please, I'll take some of everything. This looks fire."

Taji makes his plate, then hers. They both take a seat at the breakfast nook and watch Bella run around in the backyard.

"Taji, I hope you don't get offended but I didn't expect this food to smack the way that it does. I mean it looks great but I wasn't so sure that it would taste as good as it looks."

"Hell yes, I'm offended because why would you say that?"

"Because you don't look like the cooking type. I don't

mean any harm but you don't seem like the domestic type at all. You're so gorgeous. I know that you have men kissing the ground that you walk on. Shit, I figured that you could eat out every night of the week if you want on someone else's dime."

"Or my own because I do have my own money but you're right. I could eat out with someone different every night but that doesn't mean I don't know how to take care of myself. Once my father left, it was just my mama and me. She became a single mother overnight and raised me to look after myself. We shared the cooking responsibilities. She taught me everything that I know."

"Oh ok. Makes sense. Well, she taught you right because everything is cooked and seasoned to perfection. You fried the catfish hard just like I like them and the grits are so damn creamy. I need that recipe or at least tell me your secret."

"I will not. You're just going to have to come over and eat breakfast with me from time to time."

"I can do that. All I need is an invite. You already have an uninvited guest popping in from time to time. You don't need another one," Onyx giggles.

"Was that supposed to be funny, Onyx, because it's not? I'm still super pissed but it's been a little quiet lately so maybe he will leave me alone now. Maybe Reggie was paying him and once he found out that Reggie was dead, he stopped. After all, dead men don't pay. At least that's what I'm telling myself."

"That would be nice but don't let your guard down. People like this will lie in wait, hoping that you will slip up. We can't let that happen."

"You're right about that," Taji mutters as she takes her plate to the sink and begins washing dishes.

"No ma'am, you will not."

"No ma'am, I will not what, Onyx?"

"Wash those dishes. That's the least that I can do. Thank you for this great meal that you made for me. This means more than you know. You were absolutely right. I hadn't had a home cooked meal in ages. There are a few soul food joints that I would frequent out in Cali but none of them compared to that. Hats off to the chef," he says as he takes the plate out her hands and kisses her softly on the forehead.

Swooning, she walks outside on her deck to get a little fresh air and her phone rings. It's Jade.

"Good morning, Jade. What's up?"

"Nothing much. Just checking on you. How is your head feeling?"

"Girl, I honestly feel great. As if it never happened. I slept like a baby and woke up feeling like new money. Still pissed that he put his hands on me but as you know, I take a licking and keep on ticking."

"Yes, you do, girl. Resilient isn't even the word. Listen, as soon as I woke up, I felt the need to call and apologize to you about yesterday. My brother was right. I should have stayed the night and not leave you the way that I did. I'm sorry. I should have thought about what you needed in that moment but I didn't. I think that I was still just in a little bit of disbelief. I wanted to go home so badly but I have to tell you. Last night was bad. I thought that I was ok until I got to our bedroom and saw all his things hanging up in the closet. I lost it, Taji. In a way that I didn't think I ever would. I mean yes, in the moment, I hated him and what he did to us but to know that he is really gone just freaked me out."

"Sapphire and Diamond didn't know what to do. Hell, none of us did but I know that if you were here, you would have. You always know what to do when I'm running around like a chicken with my head cut off. Last night solidified that you are indeed my rock, my calm. I needed you and you needed me and we should have been together. I don't know how we could have helped each other in the moment but we always figure out a way. So again, I'm sorry, boo. I love you."

"Apology accepted but it was not needed. Girl, your husband just died. However you choose to deal with it is up to you. One day, you may want me in your space and the next day, you may not. Grief can come in waves but just know that if and when you need me, I'll be there."

"Now that I've gotten that out of the way. Can you tell me where my brother is? I bet he's still sleep. Yesterday was a lot and I know that he had to be dog tired."

"Yes, Jade. He was exhausted. He slept like a rock last night. I mean, he stayed in the same spot. I don't think that he rolled over once."

"Rolled over? Wait, did you two sleep together?"

"Before you lose your shit, nothing happened between your brother and me. I asked him to sleep with me because with all that I know about this so-called stalker, I was scared and didn't want to sleep alone. Since I'm outside I can tell you. It was not Reggie. I don't know who it is but he is still at it. He sent a picture to my phone with me lying across my bed. He knows exactly when someone comes and leaves my house. He is tapped in to the outside cameras and had one installed inside my bedroom."

"Oh my God, Taji! Are you serious?"

"Yes, I wouldn't make that shit up. Onyx disabled the one that he found in my room but there are no telling where he has them installed. Jade, this shit is for the birds. I'm not used to living in fear like this. I have to admit, and I know that I can to you, I'm usually not frazzled about anything. Not for long anyway but not knowing who's doing this has me shook to the core. Whomever it is, I hope they are ready because I am. I will fight to the death if I have to."

"I know you will but prayerfully, it does not come to that. I hope Onyx and his people are able to solve this before you have to deal with it on your own. With all those damn guns that you've got lying around there, I feel kinda bad for him because I know that you are going to Swiss cheese his ass," Jade laughs.

"And will. You know I don't play. Anyway, back to your brother, he's not sleep. He's in the house washing dishes," she mutters while letting Bella and herself back in.

CHAPTER 33

Not Ready But I Want To Be

"Washing dishes? Why is he doing that?"

"Damn, you've got so many questions, Jade. If you must know, I cooked breakfast for him."

"Don't be over there trying to woo my brother with those famous shrimp and grits. Please don't tell me that is what you made for him. No damn body on earth can resist that shit."

Taji giggles, "Yes, I cooked the shrimp and grits and he loved it."

"See, I don't like this. You've got my brother over there spending the night and shit. Now you cooking for him. I don't like this, Taji. Remember what I told you."

"Jade, shut up. It's nothing like that. It's a simple gratitude meal. Nothing more. Stop reading so much into shit. I don't have your brother hemmed up in my basement or tied to a radiator. We will be over there as soon as we get dressed. Before your nosy ass asks, and I know that you are, nothing happened. I did not do anything to him. I haven't touched a hair on his pretty little head," Taji laughs. "Now bye and see you later."

"She's on you bad I see. I'm going to go over there and tell her that I was in your kitty all night long. She's gonna be on your ass," he jokes.

"Please don't do that. I would never hear the end of it. She already threatened me last night. I had a headache and all but I remember that. She told me that if I couldn't love you properly and give you my number one spot then to leave you alone."

"Damn, you got it like that. Your niggas have numbers?"

"Don't start, Onyx. It's hard to explain."

"You don't have to explain, girl. I'm just kidding around with you. She acts like I can't determine if someone is playing around with me. I'm FBI, remember? I get paid to read people and their body language."

"Oh yeah? Well, what does my body language tell you about me?"

"It tells me that you are confident, not cocky. That you

don't like small talk. You are a get to the point kind of person. You are fiercely protective of all that you love and a natural leader. You like me, but you are still unsure of me. However, you don't want to be but you just can't get past yourself. Now that I think about it, you are a sour patch kid. You can be sweet when you want to be but downright vengeful when you feel th—."

"Ok ok," Taji says, cutting him off mid-sentence. "Most of that was right so I guess that you may know a little something."

"Anyway, Mr. Onyx, I'm going to head upstairs and get ready to go over to Jade's. You know I was thinking about what she said last night. That I could come over and stay with her for a while. I think that I'm going to do that. I'm going to stay out in the guest house though. I need my own space."

"Well, if that's what you decide, I'd be ok with that."

That's exactly what Taji does. She grabs a couple of weeks' worth of clothes and she, Onyx, and Bella head over to Jade's home. While Jade, Sapphire, and Diamond are at the funeral home, Jade lets herself in and from that moment to the next, she becomes the rock that Jade needs. Taji is there for Jade during the hard nights when Jade's reality is too much for her to handle. She is also there for the nights that Jade doesn't want to sleep alone. Taji becomes a constant shoulder for her to lean on. Helping Jade overcome grief day by day.

The creepy phone calls and text messages stop completely and Taji starts to feel a sense of normalcy again. Day after day, Taji and Onyx become closer to one another. Onyx returns from work and spends a little time with Jade. Then head straight to the guesthouse to chill with Taji until it is time for bed. They are becoming practically joined at the hip.

The closer Taji and Onyx become, the more comfortable Jade becomes with it. Taji staying in the guesthouse gives Jade the opportunity to peep how Taji is moving.

There are no more late-night excursions. There are no more freaky tales about Lucas, Malcolm, or any of the others. All Taji can focus on and talk about is Onyx and surprisingly, Jade is here for it. They even spend Thanksgiving together as one big happy family.

Jade begins therapy shortly after Teef's funeral. She asks Taji to come along. She is almost positive that she is going to tell her hell no but to her surprise, she agrees. Taji knows that it is time to get right. She cares so deeply for Onyx. She knows that he is too good of a man to let any of these hookers in ATL have him. She also takes accountability in knowing that she, too, isn't ready for a man like him.

She constantly thinks about Jade's words to her. "Leave him the fuck alone if you can't love him properly."

Those words alone make her want to be better. Not for Onyx but for herself. Having Onyx around is like having a permanent mirror in her face. In order to heal, she knows she has to face the demons of her past. She is going to have to let some things go. For starters, her aim is to forgive because she sure as hell could never forget. She knows that she needs to be better and do better but most of all, heal from her childhood traumas. With the support of Onyx and Jade, she is well on her way.

After about three weeks, Taji decides that it's time to go back home. Jade is in a much better place mentally and so is she. She tells Jade and as sad as she is to see her go, she understands. Onyx, not so much.

"Why do you have to leave, Taji? Seriously, just stay a few more days. Besides, I'm off tomorrow and you said that you would come with me to go check out some houses. I still don't know my way around the A like you do."

"And I still will. I tell you what. Why don't you grab something to wear and come home with me? Tomorrow morning, we will get up and I will take you around to different areas and realtor companies. I'll do all the driving. As long as you promise to take me to brunch."

"You've got a deal, Taji. I'm going to leave my truck here and ride with you if that's ok."

Taji thanks Jade for letting her stay in her guesthouse and Jade thanks Taji for just simply being her. Onyx, Taji, and Bella hop in her ride and head home. She pulls into the garage and grabs Bella as Onyx brings the luggage and crate inside.

"It sure does feel good to be home."

CHAPTER 34

Pressure Vs. Pipes

"I bet it does. I didn't tell you but I had the police ride by here every four hours to make sure nothing was out of place. They said everything looked normal but since you haven't been here for a while, I'm going to do a thorough search to make sure. This is a big house and there is lots of space for someone to hide."

"Thank you, love," she says as she makes her way upstairs to get a bath started. She throws her clothes to the floor and submerges her entire body in the water. Onyx arrives at her bedroom door to inform her that everything was clear.

"I've searched every inch of this place and it looks all good. I'm going to go do what you are doing and then head to bed. I will see you in the morning. Ok, babydoll?"

"Wait, can you come in and wash my back please?"

"Sure," he says as he slowly walks over to the tub. She hands him the African soap net and he begins to gently wash her neck and slowly makes his way down her back.

"Onyx, you are being too gentle. This is dirt we are fighting. You've got to get in there and put some elbow grease in it," she chuckles.

"Taji, I'm not trying to peel your skin off. This net is rough as hell and my hands are too big and heavy for all that. You won't get the opportunity to run off and tell anybody that I did anything to you," he giggles.

She grabs his hand and moves it across her shoulders. She guides him and presses into her skin, applying the perfect amount of pressure.

"See, just like that. It doesn't take much but you felt like you were barely there."

"You know I look at you like a delicate flower. You are too precious to hurt in any kind of way," he mutters as he washes her back. "Taji, I knew from the first time that I saw you that you were special. I almost didn't hear what you were saying to me when you ran down those stairs with your phone in your hand. Seeing the fear in your beautiful eyes made me think, *maybe she's saying something important so I better listen.* Immediately after that, all I've wanted to do since then is protect you and keep you safe. After Chosen did what he did to you, I was so hurt and I was so angry at myself for letting that happen."

"Do you know how crazy you sound? Onyx, none of that was your fault. I told you that he was cool and you had no choice but to take my word for it. Hell, I've known him for years and didn't know that he was capable of such things. There was no way that you could have known. Please do not blame yourself for anything, Onyx, you are the reason for everything good that is going on in my life right now. You make me want to be better, you make me want to trust, heal, and love."

"Love, Taji? Didn't you say that –"

"Shut up, I know what I said but I feel differently now. I've said it over and over that I'd never met anyone that made me want to find out what love truly is. You are *that* one. Before you, no one was worth the trouble. Now I know that sex is not required to develop feelings for someone. If anything, it can cloud your judgment. These days, I'm seeing 20/20," they both chuckle.

"I hear that, Taji. We get along so well. I mean yeah, the sexual tension is there but that can be good. We get to see how each other responds under pressure."

"Oh Onyx, you have no idea. I'm great under pressure. I do my best work," Taji laughs.

"Is that so? Let's put it to the test."

Onyx disrobes in front of her and climbs into the bathtub. Taji starts blinking 100 miles a minute.

"Now why would you do that?"

"Because you said you do your best work under pressure, so let's see what you do."

He takes the soap net from her hand and begins washing her feet. Then he travels up her leg until he reaches her inner thigh. Taji grows anxious as he closes in on her snatch. He places her toes into his mouth, sucking them one by one while still inching towards her pussy. He drops the cloth and slides two fingers deep into her snatch. She throws her head back, trying to swallow her moans, and she fails. He removes his fingers and tells her to grab the side of the tub. She does, and he reaches under her and lifts her up, bringing her pussy to his mouth. He sucks her clit and tongue fucks her until she releases every ounce of nectar she has. Onyx sops it up, slurping every drop. He lowers her back down and she reaches beneath the water and grabs his huge dick. She practically pulls him out of the water, taking him into her mouth. Attempting to relax her jaw to accommodate his width, her jaws damn near become unhinged. She is in literal disbelief. *It's like sucking on a Lysol can.*

"Boy, where did you get this big old dick from? I can barely fit it in my mouth."

"Alabama grown, baby, and you're doing fine. Take what you can, I know where to put the rest," he moans as she sucks the tip and strokes the shaft.

"Onyx, I'm trying but damn," she mutters.

"No worries, come here," he says as he sits back down in the tub. He grabs her legs, sliding her to him. He sticks his tongue out and she sucks it the way that she attempted to suck his dick. Kissing her deeply and passionately, he cuffs one of her breasts with one hand and wraps his hand around her neck with the other. Removing the hand from her breast, he guides her to his member. Taji's eyes widen from pain. Pleasure hasn't arrived yet.

"Oh my God, Onyx! Hold on, baby. You've got to take this slow."

"Taji," he whispers. "You are on top, go as slow as you need to. Just ease down on it. You are slippery enough, let the water help you."

She gasps and he gently pushes his way inside her sugar walls. Stretching her to the max. Taji pants as she struggles to slide up and down.

"That's it, baby, just take it slow," Onyx groans.

She rocks back and forth gently until she's able to take it all. Once that happens, she doesn't let up. The sensation is phenomenal. Nothing like she's ever felt before. His sheer girth and width makes her cum back-to-back. Onyx presses a button that she never even knew existed. She rides him like a seasoned cowgirl, thrashing, moaning, and groaning with every stroke. That is until he grabs her waist to assist her and starts to fuck back.

"Onyx, I... I can't," she whimpers.

"You can't what?" he whispers while looking deep into her eyes.

"Onyx, I can't!" Taji moans, biting her lip.

"Talk to me, baby, you can't what?" he questions as he grabs her by the waist, pushing her down on his dick. Her cervix quakes. It almost feels as if it's going to shatter. "Tell me Taji, tell me what you can't do?"

"I can't take it, Onyx, it's too big!"

"Yes, you can, you are, and you will," he says as the hot lava forcefully erupts from his dick. Water pours from the tub as they both explode in the best way possible. Panting, they both collapse.

"Mmmm... Taji. That's a good girl. You were right. You do work well under pressure."

"Boy, shut up and get me out of this tub. I can barely move. I will probably need a doctor after that big ole dick. Onyx, you were definitely holding out," Taji quips as they exit the bathtub.

They decide to skip the pajamas and they both climb into bed in their birthday suits. Completely exhausted from their session. They fall asleep within minutes but wake up at some point during the night for round two. Pleasuring each other until almost daybreak, they tap out again and both fall soundly asleep.

CHAPTER 35

Talk Him Through It

Taji wakes up in Onyx's arms, laying there and taking a moment to breathe in his essence. She doesn't know why but this moment feels special. She's been in the arms of many, but this felt *different*, causing her to savor the experience.

Taji stares into his face and can truly see herself doing this with him for the rest of her life. She's never envisioned that with anyone else. The thought surprises her. She smiles, kisses his hand, and gently slides out of bed, trying not to disturb his sleep. Slipping on her robe and house shoes, she grabs her pistol and phone. Then she quietly saunters downstairs to let Bella out and start a pot of coffee.

Taji sits on the deck as Bella handles her business and

ponders on how her life has drastically changed in just a matter of a few weeks. Just a little while ago she viewed men as just tools and a means to an end. Today, her reality is completely different. She thinks about all the men, good and bad, that she's encountered over the years. Her mind takes her to how it felt to wake up to Onyx's fine ass and what a time she had last night. She still can't believe that a man could dominate her the way that he did. *I think I'm in love,* she says as she laughs to herself.

Taji opens the backdoor and walks over to the coffee pot. She turns to grab a mug from the cabinet and sees a shadow out the corner of her eye. She smiles and turns around to greet Onyx a good morning but is shocked when she realizes that it is not Onyx. Her mug falls to the floor and she freezes in place.

"I've been waiting a long time to get you alone. I was like, *damn, this bitch has always got company or is never here.* You hate being alone, don't you?"

"Actually, I don't but that's none of your mutha-fuckin' business. What are you doing here and how did you find me?"

"Taji, that was easy. It ain't like you've changed your name or some shit like that. Plus, I paid your mom's house a visit while she was at work and a time or two while she was there. You take care of her bills for her, huh? What a great fucking daughter you are! Paying for all your mom's expenses with the money that you get from whoring. You know shit sure has changed. Back in the day women were wholesome. They had morals. They didn't walk out the house dressed like a fucking hooker like you do. This whole city is full of whores and tricks. I guess I don't have to wonder how you got this big ass house. Your pussy must have paid for it because I haven't seen you visit anybody's job since I've been here. Like, what do you need all this space for? So you can have room to fuck different niggas night after night?"

"Marcus, why do you give a damn what I do and what I have? What does it matter to you? Are you jealous?"

"Jealous of what, slut? You? Please!! You don't have shit for me to be jealous of. It's just you. No man, no kids, just you and a raggedy ass dog."

"Why the fuck are you here? Why are you bothering me?"

"You know why. Because of your trifling ass, I had to do hard time in prison. Bitch, I've been thinking about how I would make you pay for years."

"You are seriously crazy. Motherfucka, you are acting like I did something to you when it's really the other way around. You are the one that hurt me. I didn't put you in prison, Marcus. Your actions did. You thought that you were going to abuse me and rape me and get away with it. That's what you really thought, didn't you?"

"Taji, you know that you wanted it. I saw the way that you were looking at me. How you were jumping all over me while we were watching the movie?"

"You stupid muthafucka. What are you talking about? It was a scary damn movie!! I was scared and jumped. That's what you do when something frightens you. Since we are talking about things you know, I know some things, too. My mother forgave your Aunt Sonia and they started hanging out again. She told my mom about your little situation. Like, how you had to be moved from facility to facility to keep those niggas off your ass. Like, how every time they sewed your asshole back up, those niggas would have their way with you and rip it open again. Ms. Sonia was so sad for her nephew. The one that would never do that to me but did. She's not delusional anymore though. Eventually, she had to see you for the piece of shit that you are."

"Bitch, I'm going to enjoy this. I've been waiting on this for over 15 years now and I'm going to enjoy every second."

"Every second of what? You aren't going to touch me, Marcus, and if you value your life, you will stay right where you are," Taji yells as she raises the gun from her robe.

"Oh, bitch, you packing. Oh, so you gonna shoot me? Girl, don't you know that by the time you cock that bitch back, I'll already be on your ass?"

"I wouldn't fuck around and find out if I were you. I'm a good shot and you don't have as much time as you think. Marcus, I'm begging you to leave. Get out!!!!"

"No, bitch. I didn't come all this way to turn back now. So we are going to have to see this through."

"If you take one step, I'm going to blow a hole right through your muthafuckin' chest. Don't move, Marcus. I'm begging you."

Out of her peripheral, she sees Onyx trek down the steps. While distracted, Marcus jumps at her. She raises the gun to shoot but misses. Onyx runs over and cracks Marcus in the back of the head with the butt of his gun. Marcus falls to the floor, unconscious and bleeding, but still alive.

"What the fuck, Taji? Why didn't you yell for me?"

"I don't know. I wasn't thinking clearly, Onyx. I couldn't believe that this muthafucka was in my house. He is seriously crazy."

"This is the guy in the photos. Who is he?"

"The motherfucker that took my innocence. He raped me when I was 16 and went to jail shortly after. He's been in there forever. They were supposed to let me know when he got out but didn't. He looks nothing like he did back then. I didn't fully recognize who he was until he started talking."

"Ok, let me call the police and get him out of here."

"No."

"What do you mean *no*? This man has been making your life a living hell. He broke into your shit again and attacked you, Taji. What do you mean *no*?"

"No. This bastard is going to pay. He raped me, got me pregnant, and took my innocence. Then he has the nerve to get out and come for me. No, his ass is going to pay. Help me tie him up. I know that you know how. I'm taking his ass to the basement."

"Taji, no. I can't do that. I'm FBI. If they find out that I'm involved in unsanctioned torture, I could lose my career."

"Well, I suggest that you leave. I'll handle it myself."

"Are you serious right now?"

"Yes, as a heart attack. I want you to leave now. Go ahead and go!! I'll take care of this."

Onyx doesn't move an inch. He stands there in deep thought as Taji rambles through the kitchen drawers.

"I found them!!"

She holds up a bag of zip ties and puts them in her robe pocket. She grabs his wrist and starts dragging him to the basement.

"Onyx, seriously. If you don't want to be involved,

please leave. I will call you later. Please tell Jade that I'll be by after I handle him."

"Taji, what are you going to do to him?"

"I'm not sure just yet. Maybe pull his fingernails out one by one or maybe I should pull his teeth out with pliers. I honestly don't know yet but I'm sure that I will think of something."

"Why though? I'm sure that he was told not to come anywhere near you when he was released. All we have to do is call the police and his ass will go straight back to jail. Probably for a longer time than before. Please don't do this. Think about my sisters and their thirst for revenge and where it got them. You don't want to end up like them. You have so much to lose, Taji. Don't do this," Onyx pleads.

She pauses, dropping his arms. Tired from dragging Marcus, she takes the time to rest on the kitchen island.

"Onyx, I'm tired."

"I know you are. You just tried to drag a big ass man by yourself."

"No, not tired like that. I'm tired of men thinking that they can do what they want when they want to me and think that it's ok. Well, **it's not ok!**" she screams. "I don't understand why I'm always the target. I mind my business. I don't bother nobody who doesn't bother me, yet men constantly try to fuck over me. Well no more. I will not be anybody's victim anymore. I promised that the last time I was attacked would be the last. This muthafucka has to suffer."

"Taji, don't you know that it is not your job to make people pay? That is already being handled. I know you don't see it but it is. This brother laying here will never prosper in anything that he does. You are not the judge or the juror, Taji. You don't get to make those decisions without consequences."

"Fuck that, I am the executioner today. Who are you to tell me what I can and can't do, Onyx? You don't know all that I have been through."

Taji begins to cry. "Men don't look at women like me as equals. They only see our pretty faces and our fat asses. They don't respect us. They don't uplift us. They use and abuse us and I've had enough of that for a lifetime. No more, Onyx. No more." She says as she wipes the tears from her eyes.

"Look at this muthafucka here. If I don't kill him, he's just going to go out and hurt somebody else and probably get away with it. He has to die, Onyx. There is no other way."

Onyx walks over to Taji and wraps his arms around her and she falls to pieces. As he comforts her, she opens her eyes and sees that Marcus is no longer on the floor and is approaching Onyx from behind. Thinking fast, she pulls her gun out, pushes Onyx out of the way, and plants a bullet in the left side of Marcus's chest. He drops to the floor like a sack of potatoes.

He immediately struggles to breathe and his blood slowly starts to cover the floor.

She begins walking him through each phase of his death.

"Marcus, the bullet has entered your lungs. That is why you are struggling to breathe. In just a minute, they will fill up with blood and you will begin to suffocate and drown on your own liquid."

He gurgles while reaching for her ankles. Standing over him, she watches his eyes roll to the back of his head. She never breaks her gaze or looks away. She keeps her eyes locked on him.

"The blood has filled your lungs and once there is no more space, it will escape through your nose, your mouth, and maybe even your ears. Your heart is racing right now but don't you worry. It will slow down in just a minute."

As she observes the blood leaving his body, some of the hurt, fear, and anguish leaves hers.

"And now, the coup de grâce Marcus."

He struggles for a few more seconds until the ragged breathing stops.

"You know, I heard that the hearing was the last thing to go. I hope you hear this. You fucked with the wrong one then and now. I told you to leave me alone and not to fuck around and find out. You didn't listen and now you are on your way to hell. Make it there safely."

Looking over at Onyx, she slams the gun to the countertop.

"Now you can call the muthafuckin' police."

The End

Epilogue

After Marcus died. Taji felt that it was time for a complete reset. She hit the therapy sessions hard and really zoned in on her healing journey. She invited her mother to join in on the sessions because she, too, needed healing. All the places that were wrong in her life, she attempted to right. She changed her phone number and Lucas, Malcolm, Farod, Motion, and Chosen were officially a part of her past.

Jade remained single for a couple of years after Teef's death. She had no interest in dating. She was in her healing season as well. That was until a nice piece of white chocolate entered her life. He treats her like the queen that she is and she has never been happier. It took just eight short months after meeting white chocolate for him to propose. He saw what a great woman she was and swiftly took her off the market. She is doing great. She's no longer a slave to her job. She's living her best life and traveling the world.

Sapphire and Diamond still play no games when it comes to their baby sister or their big brother but they have their own families to worry about now. Diamond met a great man at an antique show. She fell in love, jumped the broom and moved to Ghana to start a new life. Shortly after marrying him, Diamond introduced Sapphire to one of his brothers and the rest was history. They now own and live in a compound helping broken or trapped women gain their independence. They are both doing well.

Taji married the love of her life after 2 1/2 years of dating. When Onyx proposed, the words barely rolled off his lips before she said *yes*. Like, why wait? She already had one child and was pregnant with the other. Onyx managed to fill her with "life" the very first time that they made love. She never saw it coming but wasn't mad when it arrived either. She never thought that she would, but she fell madly in love and is now a proud mother of two. Bijou and Onyx Jr. are two of the best things that ever happened to her. Onyx Sr. being the third.

Taji's mother, Jordan, left their hometown of Roseville and moved to Atlanta to be closer to her. Her daughter and new son-in-law bought her a townhouse in the area so that she could see her grandbabies whenever she wanted.

No charges were ever filed against Taji. It was an open

and closed case of self-defense. Because of what occurred, she had Onyx contact the Bureau of Prisons and use his connections to ensure that nothing like this ever happened again. She requested that if any of the others were to be released or scheduled for release, that she would be the first to be notified. She vowed to keep them updated on her contact information.

After all was said and done, Taji no longer felt comfortable living in that house and listed it for sale. Within weeks, it sold for a whopping 7.7 million dollars, which was more than triple what she paid for it. She moved closer to Jade so that little Bijou and Onyx Jr. could see their auntie any time they pleased.

Onyx is doing superb. He is well and thriving in the city of Atlanta. He did so well that he was offered another promotion at his job, in which he politely declined. His mind is focused on more things these days than work. He would rather be home with his wife and children, changing diapers and scaring monsters out of the closet.

He's a great husband, provider, and protector. Everything that Taji didn't know that she wanted or needed. Taji isn't aware but Onyx has been working behind the scenes to figure out what happened to her father. He feels like that is the last missing piece to her healing journey. She and her mother insist that he could stay wherever he was, dead or alive but Onyx curiosity won't let him leave it alone. After all, this is his children's grandfather, and he really wants to find out **_What truly happened to Indigo?_**

About the Author

L. L. Momon is an emerging author of black romance, romantic suspense novels and whatever else her mind can conceive. Her imagination is boundless. Her goal is to write the kind of stories that transcends you to the perfect time and place. She wants you to turn the television off and put your phone on DND. Grab your favorite blanket, a snack and tune out the world, even if it's just for a moment. Born and raised in the historical Tuskegee, Alabama, her mother can be credited for her love of romance novels. Learning to read at just four years old, she would often sneak and read books from her mother's Harlequin novel collection. While certainly not appropriate for a child, it kept her attention and was solely responsible for her love of reading. She is the author of Whittling Wood Part 1 and 2.

COMING SOON
　　To love the unhealed
　　His lying Tongue
　　The Sweetest Symphony

www.ingramcontent.com/pod-product-compliance
Lightning Source LLC
Chambersburg PA
CBHW031215020726
47499CB00002B/594